SNATCHED

BOOK TWO

LEA HART

DEDICATION

For My Daughters, My Heartbeat

ACKNOWLEDGEMENTS

I would like to thank Janell Parque for her editorial wisdom.

CHAPTER ONE

Rory dismissed the uneasiness churning in her chest and strode toward the SAI offices. At least it hadn't been a dead body or rat that was left on the front porch. Just a bunch of dead, decapitated roses. How big of a deal could something like that be?

Deciding the answer wouldn't immediately become evident, she focused on the man she'd met at Birdie's party. Was Max Bishop as capable as he'd appeared?

She certainly hoped so since having a stalker was about as much fun as dieting—something she firmly didn't believe in, as was evidenced by her size sixteen dresses.

Doing what she could to calm her fractured nerves, she took a deep breath and stepped up to the front door of the security company. She searched for a door handle and laughed when she couldn't find one. "Good Lord, how fancy is this place?" The sound of a whirring camera caught her attention, and she looked up, seeing a small one tucked into the corner of the door frame. The door slid open silently, and she gave a small finger wave to whoever had granted her entrance. "Okay, super fancy it is." She walked through the door and was greeted with a smile from the receptionist.

"Welcome to SAI. May I help you?"

"Yes, I'm here to meet with Max Bishop. He's expecting me; I'm Rory Basso."

"Of course. Please, have a seat, and I'll let him know you're here."

"Thank you." She glanced around and admired the luxurious furnishings. There were huge plants in the corners, some impressive original art on the walls, and a lovely Aubusson carpet beneath her feet. "Must be the real deal," she said quietly as she gazed through the thick glass wall that separated the back offices. Seeing Max take long strides in her direction instantly made her nerves settle—and then jump when she noticed he was far more attractive than she remembered.

Six feet of man candy was headed her way, and she took a second to admire the visual feast. The man was built like a bear, with his well-developed chest and broad shoulders. Add to that his dark green eyes that set off a deadly smile, and she didn't mind having a problem that he could solve.

Max ambled through the glass archway. "Hi, Rory, welcome to Security Alliance International. Let's go back to my office."

"Sounds perfect." She followed him down the hall and noticed that beneath the wool of his black slacks, he had an ass so tight, she could probably crack a walnut on it. A fantastically inappropriate train of thought to be on. But one that she didn't mind since it had an anesthetizing effect on the panic she'd been squashing for weeks.

Quietly sighing, she followed Max into his office and took a chair facing his desk. "I appreciate you taking the time to see me today."

"Of course." He settled himself in his large desk chair. "Just start when you're ready, and let me know how we can help."

She shook out her hair. "I am both scared and furious at the situation I find myself in since I abhor feeling vulnerable." Tilting her head, she frowned. "The son of a bitch who's been stalking me has somehow managed the impossible and upended my life. A part of me wants to return the favor, and I would love it if you could find him so I can." She gave him a small smile. "And between you and me, I have a heavy pan that would do the job brilliantly." She recrossed her legs, letting out a gust of air. "Sorry about that. I've been holding in that thought for a while, and it felt really good to say it aloud."

Max let out a crack of laughter. "It's never a bad idea to express your anger and frustration, so feel free to let go anytime you want."

"Oh, Max, you have no idea what that could entail." She folded her hands in her lap and wrinkled her nose. "I'm a woman who should never completely let go."

He gave her a flash of a dimple as his mouth broke into a confident smile. "Rory, I can handle whatever you've got. So feel free to...*let go*. Anytime."

She uncrossed her legs, and the only sound in the room was the hiss of her stockings as she tucked her legs together. Seeing Max's eyes darken and red slash his cheeks made her think they had somehow moved to flirting. Was that possible? Men who looked like him usually preferred women who were less complicated...and a whole lot more conciliatory.

Clearing her throat, she wiped the images of the two of them tangled together and opened her briefcase. "I'll certainly keep that in mind." She rummaged around and found what she'd been looking for. Holding up the bag that contained the notes, she frowned. "I'm hoping you can find the man who's responsible for sending me these."

Max came around his desk and took the seat next to her. "Let's see what this son of a bitch wants."

She handed him the Ziploc bag. "Where were you born? I noticed your accent yesterday at the party and can't tell where in the south you hail from."

"I'm from a small town in Georgia called Cedartown."

"A true Southern gentleman, then?"

"When the situation calls for it," he replied with the sexy arch of an eyebrow.

Silently she prayed for a situation *that* didn't call for it because seeing how much of a rapscallion he could be would certainly be interesting.

How had another inappropriate thought snuck in? Did the man possess special powers? *Of course, he doesn't!* Wiping her mind clean, she smiled. "I'm not sure why I'm asking about that right now." She smoothed out a wrinkle on her dress and vowed to focus on her stalker problem. "Before I got here, I reminded myself to be thankful there were only dead roses and not dead bodies on my front porch. Maybe I'm just distracting myself."

"Walking through our doors often makes the situation more real for our clients, so distracting yourself is completely normal." He rested his hand on her arm. "We got this, Rory. The team and I will take care of you."

"Thank you." Surprised by the excitement that his simple act of kindness produced, she looked down and cleared her throat. "It's lovely to have someone on my side." She watched his deep dimples disappear as he sat back and crossed his arms.

Goodbye sexy Max, hate to see you go.

"Should we start with the dead roses and why you thought it might've been a dead body, or is there another more egregious incident we should begin with?"

"So far, the decapitated roses are the high point," she replied with a twist of her mouth. "And for the record, I wasn't expecting a dead body; I was just happy there wasn't one. The last couple of months has taught me that anything is possible, and I'm not sure how far this person is willing to go." She sat back and crossed her arms. "Maybe you should teach me how to use a gun or a knife, so I have some options if I run into him or her. I mean...a woman should always be prepared, right?"

"I'm not saying no to your request, Rory."

"But you're not saying yes, either."

"Let's keep it on the back burner for now." Max returned to his desk. "We can certainly give you instructions on self-defense, but it might be best to take advantage of the multi-million-dollar training we've received and let the team handle the weaponry for the time being." He sat back and chuckled. "But, I'm guessing the blood-thirsty look in your eyes isn't going to allow that. Should I be concerned?"

Rory waved her hand in dismissal. "You seem too muscly and capable to be worried about anything." She straightened the stapler and jar of pens on Max's desk. "I think now is as good a time as any to learn how to use a small gun. Perhaps a cute one that can fit in my purse. That way, if you're busy, I can take the guy out." A smile touched her lips as she envisioned what it would be like to take control of her life and teach the stalker a lesson.

"Let's wait on the firearms training and see what we're dealing with first. After all, we want to equip you with just the right arsenal."

"Oh, I like the idea of an arsenal." She moved his tape dispenser. "Because between you and me," she pursed her lips, "I'm tired of being a victim and would very much like to dispense a little retribution."

"Totally understandable; just give me as much information as you can, and we'll make sure no one disturbs one hair on that beautiful head of yours."

She mentally pulled up her big-girl panties and gave Max a nod. "It started a couple of months ago when I was photographed with my mom, her husband, and his son. My stepfather owns about a dozen hotels around the world and is quite wealthy. The picture showed up in the newspaper, and I was listed as one of Bob's children. I never thought much about it until I received a note several days later at the office. I'm in charge of operations for all the hotels and work at the corporate headquarters in La Jolla.

"After I received threatening notes steadily for two weeks, I decided to speak with the corporate security team to see if they could put an end to it. They conducted a preliminary investigation and came up with nothing conclusive. The following month, I started receiving notes on my car as well as e-mails. My mom and I went to the police and asked for their help, but they said they couldn't do anything until the stalker contacted me in person.

"Tired of not getting anywhere, I took a last-minute business trip and traveled to all the hotel locations internationally. I figured that whoever was harassing me would lose interest, and I would get a break."

"Guessing that's not what happened."

Rory chewed her bottom lip. "It got worse. I continued to receive e-mails, and my scary stalker knew exactly where I was and let me know they could get to me anytime. Luckily, I spoke to Birdie soon after, and voila." She snapped her fingers. "Here I am with you…my new favorite security professional who will keep me safe."

"I'll be happy to do exactly that. No one will ever threaten you again. Not on my watch."

Rory leaned forward and almost fell into Max's confidence. "You make it sound so easy. I suppose that I should've come to you earlier." She handed him a flash drive with a copy of the e-mails. "I downloaded all the electronic correspondence and hope you will find it helpful." She waved to the plastic bag on Max's desk. "A few notes are missing since Bob's security team kept a few, as did the detective. I think there's enough there, though, to give you a clear picture of what I've been dealing with."

Max opened the bag and took out the ten envelopes that contained the notes. He arranged them by date and started going through them. "I wish we had more clients like you. You've done the work for us by putting them in order."

She watched him frown as he went through them and prayed he'd meant what he said. Because as much as she wanted to handle it on her own, she knew it was no longer possible.

"Why the hell has no one taken this seriously?"

Her eyes flew to his. "Everyone told me there wasn't anything actionable."

"Bullshit! The tone and threats are escalated with each subsequent note. Anyone with half a brain should be able to see the next step this guy makes is going to be violent."

"The e-mails are worse."

Max gave her a long stare. "This person wants to snatch you, and I'm sure as shit not going to let that happen."

"Really?" Her heart rate sped up. "Snatch as in take?"

"Yes, Rory. There is no mistaking this person's intent. He or she is obsessed and is ready to do some real harm." He ran his hand over his jaw. "I'm assigning a twenty-four-hour security detail. We will secure your home and car and dig through your computer and phone for clues. Whoever is after you must have left some breadcrumbs, and we'll find them." Max put the notes back in order and slid them into the bag. "Tell me about the flowers that you received this morning."

"When I walked out my front door this morning, I discovered a bunch of dead, decapitated roses." She opened her purse, pulled out the note that came with them, and handed it over. "This came with the bouquet. Not quite the missive I was hoping for, and quite frankly, I think it's rude to give someone a gift and then threaten to chop them up. He could've just skipped the flowers if all he wanted to do was make promises of maiming."

Max gave Rory a pained look, unfolded the note, and read it. "We will be placing you under twenty-four-hour protection today."

"Are you sure I'm going to need all of that?"

"Absolutely. The son of a bitch probably has eyes on you 24/7. People who do this are pushing the boundaries until you push back. They take one step forward and then another. We're going to stop this and make sure he never gets close enough to lay one finger on you."

"Well, let's get started then because I'd like to go back to my regularly scheduled life as soon as possible."

"I'm going to call my partner in and have him work on this as well." He pushed a button on his phone. "Frank, can you come into my office? Rory is here."

She heard a grunt and then watched a man walk through the side door of Max's office. Good Lord, was every man who worked here worthy of a modeling contract?

"This is Frank. He's my partner and a damn near genius when it comes to unraveling mysteries."

Rory stood and took the too handsome man's outstretched hand. "Lovely to meet you."

"And you too." Frank looked at Max and then back at Rory. "You two are going to be great together."

"What the hell are you talking about?" Max barked as he stood.

Frank chuckled. "Oh…are we pretending there isn't a line of electricity running between you two?"

"We are not pretending anything," Max thundered. "You have lost your damn mind."

"Not a person alive who doesn't already know that," Frank replied with a laugh. "But don't dismiss my gypsy fortune-telling abilities because of it. Crazy genius is not the only thing that defines me."

"Do you really have gypsy blood?" Rory asked.

Frank held his hands wide and grinned. "You tell me."

She gave the dark prince a slow once-over and then smiled. "I don't know why I asked. You clearly come from a long line of soothsayers."

Frank gave Rory a wink and then turned to Max. "This one, I like."

"If you two are done with your genetic lottery discussion, why don't we get started on finding out who's harassing Rory?"

"Party pooper," Rory said with a laugh before she handed her electronics to Frank.

"Thanks, doll. I'm going to need your car and house keys, too. We'll send your car over to the garage so we can see if it's been tampered with and then send a team to the house to install a security system."

"Really?" Rory squeaked.

"Really," Max said as he walked around the desk. "This is a serious situation, and we're treating it accordingly."

"Alright," she murmured before digging into her purse and handing her keys to Frank. "I think this is a bit much, though."

"Not even a little," Max replied.

Frank gave a short wave and then headed toward the side door. "I'll check back and let you know what we come up with."

She watched him walk out of the office and wondered what she had put in motion.

"Do you have a gut feeling about who this person might be?"

She looked up at Max's looming presence and shook her head. "Not a clue. I interact with a lot of people and wouldn't know where to start."

Max took the chair next to Rory's. "Tell me about work and any ex-boyfriends."

She let out a sigh. "Well, no ex-boyfriends are lurking around since I haven't had one in years."

"Okay, that's good news. Tell me about work."

"Why is that good news?"

"Because spurned lovers and boyfriends tend to be the most violent. A man who's had his heart or ego broken can be unpredictable." He took her hand. "And I'm guessing that any man that fell for you would be inconsolable."

"Oh," she said quietly, realizing that Frank had been right. There was electricity between them. "That's a lovely thing to say."

"So, anyway...tell me about your job."

She blinked twice and slipped her hand away. "I went to work for Bob after I graduated from college. I planned on spending a year with the hotels to gain some experience and then move on. I've been there for six years and think it's time to make a change."

"Because of the stalker situation?"

"Not necessarily."

"Don't let anything scare you away from a job you like. This will be over before you know it, and there's no reason to make major changes to your life."

"I might be ready for some major changes, no matter how this thing turns out." Playing with her bracelets, she shrugged. "Truth is, I'm good at my job but don't enjoy it. I'm tired of dealing with Bob's son, and this stalker thing might be the perfect excuse to make a move."

"Tell me about your step-brother. Has he always given you a hard time?"

"He's not my step-brother; he's Bob's son. When your mother gets remarried while you're in college, you do not acquire siblings. And for the record, Jackson is a jerk and a narcissist who tends to exhibit erratic behavior quite regularly. He's resented me since his father gave me a job, and I've always had the impression that he believes the world is a zero-sum game."

"We'll take a look at him." Max stood and started pacing. "Do you want to make a job change right away?"

"I'm ready to give my notice but will stay if you think it will help catch the creep who's been harassing me."

"Let's keep your routine the same while we gather information."

"Okay, Max. I'm ready to follow your lead."

"Nothing I like better." He stopped pacing and crossed his arms.

She felt a smile form as she felt the hundred-pound weight she had become familiar with slip into the man's promises of protection. "I'm starting to feel relieved." Letting out a laugh, she gazed at Max. "I'm ready to create something completely new." She arched an eyebrow. "And, if you can get me a gun and show me how to use it, I might feel even better."

"How long have you had this desire for firearms?"

She swallowed and let her gaze drop to his mouth, thinking about what desire would look like with Max. Heat and excitement pinged to life, and she couldn't believe after all this time it was this burly bear of a man who made it possible. "I…uuhhh just decided today." She studied her nails and hoped he couldn't read energy like his buddy because the last thing she needed was for him to figure out exactly what kind of pictures were dancing across her imagination.

"You okay, Rory?" He strode to her side and took her hand. "I don't want you to worry anymore. I'm going to handle this."

Pictures of what that might look like filled her brain, and before she could fully let them develop, the phone buzzed, and Frank's voice came across the intercom. "You should get that." Clearing her throat, she unlaced their hands and stood. "Which way to the ladies' room?"

Max stepped back. "Down the hall, last door on the left."

"Thanks." She walked out of the office and took a big breath. Max Bishop was like no other man she'd ever met, and the things she wanted to do with him were downright naughty.

Sighing, she told herself to focus on what was important. She passed a large office with screens covering the walls and noticed several men hunched over keyboards as data scrolled across the monitors. Having access to that much information was a powerful asset, and she hoped it would be made available to end this stalker thing once and for all.

It was time to begin a new life, and the sooner she could get started, the better.

CHAPTER TWO

Max finished with his call and then went in search of Rory. Heading in the direction of the back offices, he turned the corner and caught sight of her as a swirl of anticipation kicked him deep in the gut.

It was sexual energy combined with something else…something deeper and more complicated. His pulse quickened as he stepped closer and took her hand. "I came to find you. Lunch is going to be delivered to the conference room in a few moments."

Standing in the middle of the hallway, the noise of the office fell away, and he didn't know what he was supposed to do with the slam of chemistry. He was a professional—always had been. He'd never stepped across a line, but he sure as hell wanted to with the woman standing before him. And once he was over that line, he wanted to…hold on—a feeling he could confidently say that he'd never experienced before.

Desire clanged through his body, and he knew that stopping it or ignoring it was going to be damn near impossible. "Are you hungry?"

"Oh…well, I suppose a little."

"Well, then, let me take care of that for you." Putting his hand on the small of her back, he led her into the conference room. More than half the table was covered with large platters of sandwiches, various salads, and bowls of chips. "I hope we've got something you like." He glanced down. "If not, let me know and we can order whatever you like."

"That won't be necessary." Rory swept her hand over the table. "Are you feeding an army?"

"Not an army, just a bunch of retired SEALs. We like to eat, and I've found that it's a good idea to keep the team happy." He pulled out a chair and tucked her in. "What would you like to drink?"

"Water would be great, thank you."

He brought her a bottle and took a seat. "We're getting a handle on the situation and have a preliminary TAC plan in place." Silently congratulating himself for stringing words into a sentence, he felt confident that he had everything under control.

"What is a TAC plan?"

"That's short for a tactical plan—the way we're going to approach solving this issue for you." He opened a bottle of iced tea, took a big slug, and then felt the heat of her gaze. Liking her full attention, he fell into her warm smile and accepted that his SOP was about to change. Rory Basso wasn't going to be like any other client, and his standard operating procedure was due for an update.

"Is everyone who works here a former Navy SEAL?"

"Once a SEAL, always one. We're either active or retired, and yes, most of the key operators are retired from the Teams. We've all worked with one another at some point in our careers and speak the same language. You could put two SEALs that have never met on an op, and they would be operating as a team in less than a minute, which, for the record, is the secret to our company's success." He sat back and noticed her eyes were glued to his. "Are you doing okay? I know this is a lot to take in."

"I'm great. Knowing that I can tip this problem into your very capable hands is such a relief."

"My hands can handle whatever you got, Rory." Her eyes flared, and he realized how inappropriate the comment sounded. "What I meant…"

"It's fine, Max. I like the idea of having you on my side."

"Good. That's real good."

Since I'm not gonna let any other son of a bitch near you.

A thought that crossed the line of professionalism in about a dozen different ways.

Before he could decide what to do about it, the door opened, and five team members entered in a rush. Max watched them fill their plates and then settle in at the table.

"Are all of them here for me?"

"Of course." Max gave her a wink and stood. "Thanks for jumping on this, guys; after we're done eating, let's tell Rory how we're going to go after this threat."

He filled two plates quickly and then returned to his seat. "Does that look okay?"

"Yes," Rory mumbled as she looked around the room.

"Team guys operate best together. Each man here has a specialty, and we get as much input as we can before putting a plan together."

Frank walked in and took a seat next to Max. "We have some decent leads from Rory's computer. Derick will fill everyone in after we eat lunch."

Max nodded and then noticed Rory picking at her food. Leaning over, he draped his arm across the back of her chair. "You can let some of your worries go because I yield to no one, and the same can be said for all the operators in this room."

"Thank you," she murmured. "Seeing everyone assembled makes me feel like the threat was bigger than I imagined."

He curved his shoulders inward as he turned, creating a little wall of privacy. "It's nothing we can't handle." He lifted a fork and handed it to her. "Eat something, please." He gave her a long look and noticed that her beautiful emerald eyes were decorated with flecks of gold. The woman was a stunner, and she also happened to be brave as hell and whip-smart—qualities that he didn't know how to ignore.

Rory set down the fork. "I guess that I'm not hungry, after all."

He dipped his head, so they were eye to eye. "Someone will have to get through me to get to you, and that's never going to happen."

Rory shivered. "I guess there isn't much more that I could ask for."

He took her hand and told himself it was a gesture of comfort. When he felt the beat of her heart against his, he knew that he was offering her a lot more than professional compassion.

Was she the one he'd been looking for?

Hearing Frank whistle made him pull his focus together, and he sat up. "Here we go."

Frank tapped the table with a pen. "Let me give you what we have so far, and then we can get everyone's input." He filled the team in and then nodded to Derick.

"Someone has installed a worm on Rory's computer," Derick said quietly. "They have access to the system and have full control of the camera. So not only is this son of a bitch smart but creepy." He turned to Rory. "The asshole has also accessed your cell phone by cloning your password."

Rory stilled, and Max tightened his hold. "Breathe, Rory."

Derick continued, "I have installed the appropriate countermeasures, and I'm close to getting an IP address. I should have some info by the end of the day. Clearly, the guy is obsessed, and hijacking the camera suggests it's personal and not financially motivated. But I need to do more research before I rule that out completely."

Frank looked up from his phone. "There was a tracker on your car, and the guys said it wasn't a sophisticated device, which is good news because we likely have someone with advanced computer skills and little else. They've taken it out and replaced it with one of our GPS devices. We've also sent a team to your house, and they've started on your system."

"Thank you very much," Rory said as she sat up. "It's a lot to take in, and I'd be lying if I didn't admit how freaked out I am." She shook her head. "I think if someone sees you in your panties, they should at least be willing to buy you a drink." She looked around the table. "Am I right on this?"

The room erupted in laughter, and Max stood. "Thanks for the input, men; we'll circle back together in the morning and put the final plan in place." He put his hand out to Rory and helped her out of her seat, and then led her into his office and closed the door.

***

Rory strode into Max's office and fisted her hands. "Someone saw me naked; I always leave my laptop open when I'm traveling."

"The good news is that it will never happen again. The bad news is that I'm not going to be polite when I come face-to-face with the person responsible."

"Are we sure that's possible?"

"Which part?"

"The face-to-face part?"

"Absolutely, we're very good at what we do."

Rory started pacing. "I think we can now both agree that a gun is necessary."

"What if I'm your arsenal?" Max gave her a confident smile. "Would that make you feel better?"

"No, I want to be able to defend myself." She stopped moving. "You're not going to be with me every day."

"Yes, I am, Rory."

"What?" She looked from side to side. "How is that possible?"

"I'm going to be your twenty-four-hour bodyguard. We're about to become peanut butter and jelly."

"But…"

Max cut Rory off as she was about to turn. "Someone's got to do it. And I'm the best option."

"It's just that…"

Max's eyebrows slammed down over his eyes. "You want one of the other guys on your six?"

"I might be better able to answer that question if I knew what a six was."

"It means your back. I go where you go and vice versa."

Rory stepped back and bit her bottom lip. "I'm not sure that you and I…together is such a good idea."

"Really?" he asked, rocking back on his heels. "You think Frank or Derick is a better option?"

Not caring for the tone Max was taking, she narrowed her gaze. "Yes, as a matter of fact, I do!"

"Why?" he asked in a sharp tone.

Rory flapped her hands. "Because I don't want to kiss them!" Max lifted her hand, and she groaned when she saw a satisfied smile decorate his stupidly handsome face. "If you start gloating…"

"Honey, this is not gloating."

"Well, what is it?"

"The very definition of full-freaking happiness."

"Oh…" she looked up and pinched her mouth together. "It looks suspiciously similar to self-satisfaction."

"There is only one way to find out."

"And that is?" Seeing him move in and lower his head made her stomach flip-flop. "What are you doing?"

"Showing you that what I say is what I mean."

Not prepared in any way, Rory moved closer and gripped a handful of Max's perfect white shirt in her hands. His mouth fell against hers in the gentlest kiss. It was almost innocent and so beautiful; it pinched a corner of her heart.

Was it wrong to kiss one's bodyguard?

Well, too bad if it were because there was no way she could muster a decent objection if there'd been a gun to her head.

Max Bishop could kiss her anytime he felt like it. She completely and, for the record, thoroughly enjoyed his lips on hers. It was like coming into fleeting contact with something incredibly powerful—something that could burn if the contact were too close. "Is this your way of distracting me from my problems or showing me how you're going to take care of me?"

"Yes to both." He wrapped his arms around her and kissed her again.

The hum of power coming off of him was almost audible.

Sliding into the euphoria, she almost missed the sound of the side door opening and Frank's laughter.

"I thought you guys would wait until tomorrow before you started smooching. This is a place of business."

"Get out," Max grumbled as he tore his mouth away from Rory's.

The sound of laughter filled the office until Frank left and closed the door. "So, I guess you can be my bodyguard."

"Good, because I didn't want to resort to hinky tactics."

Rory stepped back and straightened her dress. "We can discuss hinky shenanigans later."

"Might be best if we save that conversation until we're alone."

"Are you looking smug again?"

"No, woman." Max walked around his desk and collapsed into his chair. "This is me being knocked on my ass."

"Okay, that's good." She slid her thumb across her bottom lip and decided that he did appear to be a little gobsmacked.

Perhaps he was smarter than she suspected and understood that wild sexual attraction was the most dangerous thing on earth. It was a loaded grenade, in fact, and the sooner they recognized it, the better.

"Just as a point of clarification…do you kiss all your distressed female clients?"

"No! What do you take me for?"

"A man who knows what he wants and doesn't stop until he gets it." She flipped her hair over her shoulder and knew that she had nailed him perfectly. "So, what do we do now?"

"Would you like me to take you to your office for a couple of hours?"

Rory looked from side to side and then let out a short laugh. "That's not what I thought you were going to say."

Max ran his hand over the top of his desk. "If you have another idea, I'd be happy to discuss it."

"You behave, Max Bishop."

"Wasn't planning *not* to."

"And yet, the gleam in your eye suggests otherwise."

"I'm keeping that gleam for later."

"Noted." She collapsed into a chair. "I think showing my face at the corporate offices would be a good idea. I can take a cab, though, since I'm sure you're quite busy."

"You remember the part about us becoming cheese and crackers?"

"I thought it was peanut butter and jelly."

"Same idea."

She fiddled with her sleeve. "How are we going to explain your presence? It's not like I show up at the office in the middle of the day with a handsome hunk on my arm."

Max grinned. "Easy. I'm your new boyfriend."

"I don't have boyfriends; no one's going to believe that."

"Why not?"

"Because I don't."

"As clear of an answer as that is, I'm gonna need some clarification."

"You do not need to know about my love life. That's not why I've acquired a stalker."

"Are you sure?"

"Well, of course, I'm not sure." She put her hands on her hips and stared him down. When he didn't immediately shrink, she wondered if she'd lost her magic powers. She let out a little huff and tried again. Nothing.

Well, that was going to be inconvenient.

"You done?"

"No…I was going to…oh, never mind." She let her shoulders drop. What were we talking about?"

"Us. Enamored." He gave Rory a confident grin. "Not being able to keep our…"

"Enough, I get the picture."

"Nothing wrong with a little uncontrolled lust, Rory. Not only because we're likely to enjoy the hell out of it, but because us showing the world our fire might shake the trees and inspire the asshole harassing you to slip up and reveal himself."

"You just made that up."

"I did not."

Smirking, she rolled her eyes. "That is a tiny truth wrapped up in a big fat fib."

"And your point is?"

"I have no idea."

"We might as well get used to it because as far as I can tell, that's going to be our SOP going forward."

Too exhausted to ask which sexual position he was referring to, she gave him a bland smile and prayed that her mother was nowhere near when she broke all ten of the commandments.

CHAPTER THREE

Max piloted his SUV through La Jolla and wondered if the hot, dry weather was a precursor to anything important. The Santa Ana winds had been blowing all week, and he knew that meant people were acting crazier than usual.

It was going to be interesting to see who was going to let their freak flag fly. Glancing over, he studied the quiet woman in his passenger seat. "How are you doing?"

"Okay, considering what's going on." She opened one eye and then leaned back. "How are you doing?"

"Good." He took Rory's hand and then shook his head. "No, make that great."

She lifted their clasped hands. "Is this part of our security strategy?"

"No, I just like holding your hand." He rested their clasped hands on his leg. "I'm attracted to you and have decided not to fight it. I'm not going to play games or act like I don't care. In fact, I'm going to lean into it. I'm thirty-eight years old and understand how rare it is to have a woman like you show up in my life."

"Well...that's..."

"A lot to take in. I know." He tapped his brakes as they hit a pocket of traffic and then looked over, seeing that she'd closed her eyes. "Have you gone to your happy place?"

"Yes," she replied quietly. "I'm mentally walking around Nieman Marcus in Fashion Valley and admiring all the pretty strappy sandals."

"Well, I won't disturb you then."

"Thank you and know that I've just given you a gold star for understanding the importance of retail therapy."

He squeezed her hand and didn't know why the statement made him so flipping happy. He had a box full of medals in the back of his closet and more letters of commendation than he could count, and none of them felt as good as Rory's gold star.

As they rolled down the highway, he tried to understand why she was the one who crossed his heart. What was it about the woman that had half his synapses going offline and his body reverting to its teenage hormonal insanity?

Averting his eyes from the road, he grabbed a glance and knew that discovering the reasons was not only going to be fun but a mission of a lifetime.

Twenty minutes later, he stood next to Rory on the elevator and watched her hands twist together. "I will handle this for you, Rory. No matter what. Whoever wants to get at you is going to have to go through me first."

Looking up, she held his gaze. "I doubt that anything has ever gotten through you." She waved her hand. "How do you do that?"

"What," he asked with curiosity.

"The moment we traversed the parking lot, your energy completely changed, and you went on high alert. I felt like I was watching some transformer trick. You went from corporate mucky-muck to soldier. The air around you is supercharged, and I think you might've somehow grown bigger...and more menacing."

"Party trick," he replied quietly. "I'm most comfortable in the middle of a conflict and like to maintain a combat-ready approach." He took her hand. "Lucky for you, it's going to keep you out of the hands of someone who wants to do you harm."

"I suppose so," she mumbled quietly as the doors slipped open and they stepped off the elevator.

Max followed Rory down the hall and guessed that she wasn't ready for a complete picture of how being under his protection would look. They approached a group of four offices, and she turned into the first one, flipped on the lights, and set down her stuff. When she glanced up, he motioned for her not to say anything.

He pulled out a scanner and swept the office for bugs. Interestingly enough, he found an audio device on a picture frame and a mini camera in a plant on her desk. Knocking the plant over, he grabbed the mini camera and crushed it under his boot. "Sorry about that, honey." She gave him a confused look and held up her hands. He mimed a camera and then put his finger to his mouth.

"Don't worry about it. I'll call housekeeping later and have them clean it up."

"Why don't you give me a tour before I do any more damage?"

"Good idea," she said with a shake of her head. "Let me introduce you around."

He grabbed her hand as they walked down the hall and noticed it was clammy—a fact that made him vow silently to end the harassment by week's end.

Rory introduced Max to her assistant and two other department heads and then knocked on the last office door before pushing it open. "Jackson, do you have a couple of minutes? I want to introduce you to Max."

They entered a big corner office, and a tall blond man sat behind a desk with paperwork spread across it. "Hello, Rory. I didn't realize that you were back in town."

"I returned last Friday from Europe. I'll send you a copy of my report by the end of the week."

Max noticed that her hold tightened on his hand and wondered if she realized what she was doing. *What the hell has this guy done to her?*

Stepping forward, he held out his hand and watched the confusion color the man's face. "I'm Max Bishop, Rory's boyfriend." He received a fake smile in response and a short shake of his hand. Not able to stop himself, he gave the man a combat stare and watched him pale under his tan. Men usually recognized the alpha in the pack, and he wasn't surprised to see the man catch on so quickly.

Max stepped back and wrapped his arm around Rory. "I wanted to see where Rory worked and meet some of the people that she spends her day with." Waiting silently, he remained still. *Ball is in your court, asshole. Let's see what you're going to do.*

"Rory, I didn't realize that you're seeing someone. Where did you two meet?"

"I met Max through my friend Birdie. She's engaged to Mark Frazier, a Lt. Commander on Team One. He and Max used to work together." She looked up and gave Max a wide smile. "Max retired from the Teams a couple of years ago and has a security firm in downtown San Diego."

She wrapped her arm around his waist and sighed. "I met him and knew. It's not every day a man like Max comes into your life. Anyway, we won't keep you." Stepping back, she tugged on Max's hand. "I'll follow up with you later in the week."

"Okay, that's fine...so, Max, how long were you a SEAL?"

"Once a SEAL, always one," Max replied. "I was on the Teams for fifteen years and have been retired for two. Did you ever serve?" He knew damn well this guy had never served anyone but himself and couldn't resist making a point. This was a game of chess, and they were moving their pieces around with each sentence.

"No, I didn't." He sat back with a noxious haze of self-importance. "I've been working for my father since I graduated college and have learned the business from the ground up. I'm going to take the company to the next level very soon."

Max nodded. "Well, we'd better let you get back to that...big plan."

"Are you ready, sweetheart?" Rory asked with enough sugar to make sweet tea. "I want to introduce you to some of my friends."

"Can't wait," he said before following her out of the office. Males, above all, are animals—herd animals with a keen instinct for when to stay out of the alpha's way. Thankfully, the five-minute chat he'd just had with Jackson established who was who, and Max appreciated that it had taken so little effort.

"I enjoyed the nature show," Rory said quietly. "It's not often you get to see something like that in real-life."

"Glad you enjoyed it." He rolled his shoulders. "We just made our first move across the board;

hopefully, it will net some valuable intel by day's end."

"Indeed," Rory said quietly.

They continued the tour, and by the time they were done, Max had about five people he was interested in looking at further. All in all, a fruitful recon exercise. "Thanks for showing me around. Do you have time to walk me outside?"

"Of course."

They were standing in front of the tall glass building five minutes later, and he took Rory's hands. "I've got some strong leads, so rest easy; we'll have this wrapped up before you know it."

"Really?" She raised her eyes to the building. "It almost seems too easy. Do you think my stalker is up there, plotting their next move?"

"Yes. Whoever is harassing you has access to your office, your computer, car, and phone. The only way that's possible is if they work for your company."

Running her hand along her arm, she bit her lip. "I'm officially more creeped out—something I hadn't thought possible."

Max studied her worried eyes and dropped his mouth to her ear. "I'm gonna kiss you in a minute and want to know if you're okay with it."

"Well, I...uhhh..."

"I want to make sure that whoever has you in their sights knows that you are not alone."

"That makes sense."

"I also enjoyed the hell out of our earlier kisses and wouldn't mind grabbing a couple before I leave."

Rory moved closer and laid her hand on his cheek. "Then, let's make it a good show."

"Yes, ma'am." He pressed their mouths together and slicked his tongue along her bottom lip. A guttural satisfaction filled his chest, and he wished that they weren't in public, and he could kiss her like he wanted to. Reminding himself that patience was his greatest ally, he released her mouth. "I think that did the job."

"It certainly did," she said in a quiet voice. "I felt that kiss everywhere."

"Same." Clearing his throat, he took a half-step back. "I'll be back in a couple of hours to pick you up. Keep your head on a swivel and trust no one."

"That seems a little dramatic."

"Not even a little." He glanced up and shook his head. "See what you can do about working off-site. I don't like the idea of you being in there alone after today."

"Alright, but…"

"Rory, this situation doesn't allow for buts. Someone wants to harm you, and I don't plan on letting that happen."

"Okay, Max. We will do this your way."

Bending down, he kissed her cheek. "Appreciate the cooperation."

"Considering you're keeping me out of harm's way, it's not that hard."

Trying not to picture the hard parts, he cleared his throat and moved away. "Be back in two hours."

Rory blew a kiss. "Can't wait."

He chuckled and enjoyed the view as Rory walked back toward the building. The world had finally served up his match, and he couldn't believe how freaking happy the concept made him. He never really expected to find someone, and to have finally come face-to-face with a woman that embodied all the things he desired was humbling.

Rory Basso was everything he could hope for and more.

No doubt about it, he was the luckiest son of a bitch in the world.

CHAPTER FOUR

Later that evening, Rory walked through the door of her little house and noticed several SAI team members were still working. "Max, I'm going to change, and then I'll start dinner."

"Okay, honey."

Waving to three men as she passed, she stepped into her room and closed the door firmly. She flopped on her bed and let out a sigh. "Sayonara quiet life." The day's trifecta of a stalker, thoughts of a job change, and a delicious man declaring his intentions washed over her tired body. It was a lot to take in, and she didn't think just one glass of alcohol was going to make it better. A short knock on her door made her lift her head. "If you don't have a glass of wine in your hand, please go away."

Max opened the door slowly. "What kind of wine do you want?"

She dropped her head back to the bed. "There's a bottle in the fridge, and the glasses are in the cupboard. Help yourself to whatever you want, and please offer something to the guys as well."

"Roger that. Be back in five."

Before he cleared the door, she threw him a smile. "I like this whole following orders thing you're doing."

"Not a surprise."

She heard Max's laughter as he walked out of the room and decided he owned one of the world's finest tushies. Certainly, not enjoying the view would be a direct insult to God.

A sin she wasn't interested in committing given her current predicament.

She pushed herself off the bed and slipped off her high heels. "Better." Another knock made her turn toward the door. "Come in."

"As requested."

"You are a good human, Max." She took the glass and held it up. "To superheroes that deliver libations."

"Oh honey, I plan on delivering a lot more than that."

"Oh…well…that's good news…"

"I'm hoping so." He lifted his hand. "Need help with a zipper or anything?"

"With a houseful of strangers?"

"I wasn't…what I mean is…"

Rory set her glass down and pressed her hand to Max's enormous chest. "Did I just fluster a commander in the Navy?"

"Of course not," he replied roughly, squaring his shoulders. "I am always in control."

She pushed her mouth together. "That's too bad because I kind of like the idea of affecting someone as strong as you."

Max tilted her chin with his thumb. "Make no mistake, woman; you affect me in ways I have yet to understand. But I'm not gonna be flustered." He shook his head. "I'll be insatiable and unable to stop until we're both breathlessly spent and satisfied."

Rocketed by his words, she nodded and hoped that it was possible. She'd heard just about every promise, declaration, and testimony of what a man thought he could deliver and had yet to see any of it come to fruition.

A river of cynicism ran through her veins, and until she saw the proof in the pudding, she wasn't going to hold her breath. Even if the formidable man holding her hands seemed capable of delivering on every promise he made. "I will keep that in mind." She gave him a sassy smile and then turned toward her closet. "I will be out in a little bit."

"And, I'll be waiting."

She stepped into her sanctuary and heard the door snick closed. Was she truly ready to see if a man like Max was the real deal?

It was a question that she wasn't quite ready to answer.

Fifteen minutes later, she walked out and heard nothing but silence. How had the team finished so quickly?

She strolled into the living room and knew the man standing in the center of it was going to test every single one of her theories about relations between the sexes. "Where did everyone go? I was going to make dinner for the team."

Max turned and sucked in a breath. "Good God, woman, you've got to warn a man before you show up like that."

Looking down, she let out a snort. "I didn't know yoga pants, a T-shirt, and my hair piled high on my head was a reason for a news alert."

Stalking closer, he let out a whistle. "How is this version sexier than the dressed-up one?"

"It's not, and I wonder if now wouldn't be the time to have your vision checked."

"I can see perfectly." He took her hand. "Tell me what you're hungry for, and I'll run out and get it."

"I can make something...pasta or..."

"You've had a hell of a day, and I think you should take the night off." He stepped in. "Let me do this."

There were quite a few things she would let the man do, and grabbing food was probably the safest. "Do you like Chinese?"

"Love it."

"I'll call an order in and then grab a jacket. We can go together."

Okay, but if you want to stay home, you'll be secure. We've installed a system that won't allow a squirrel to cross the perimeter without us knowing."

"Really?"

"Yes. We believe more is better and never cut corners when we can add them."

"Well, it would be nice to put my feet up and take a minute to process everything."

Max kissed her hand and then handed over his phone. "Make the call and then process to your heart's content."

"You are too good to be true, Max Bishop." And she meant it because, as far as she could tell, the man was the real deal. His strength didn't come from his muscles or bravado but from his integrity and a clear commitment to doing the right thing.

A combination that would be all but impossible to resist.

***

Max sat at Rory's dining table and pushed his plate back. "How are you doing? Are you in overload yet?"

Rory lifted her glass and emptied the dregs of her wine. "I can't tell, which is probably an indication that I'm floating in the River Denial." She swept some crumbs into her hand. "I've told myself for months that this thing was an irritant and not a real threat, but spending the day with you shows me how foolish that was. There's someone out there who will do me harm if given half a chance."

He leaned forward and covered her hand. "I'm glad that you're taking this seriously and want to tell you again that we've got you covered. No one will get to you."

"Speaking of covered, I need to write you a check for your services." Just as she was about to push away from the table, she saw her bodyguard shake his head. "What's with the look of disapproval?"

"I'm not charging you." He sat back and crossed his arms across his chest. "We're doing this for free."

"That's crazy, Max. The round-the-clock protection and fancy security system are worth at least ten thousand right out of the gate."

"I said what I said. No charge."

"Absolutely not." She stood and grabbed her purse. "If you don't accept remuneration, I will find another company that will."

"Over my dead body," he barked. Pushing himself to his feet, he took her purse and set it on the counter. "This is my company, and I do business as I see fit. Keeping women out of harm's way at no charge is something that we've always done and will continue to do. We're wildly successful, and I am sharing our resources with those who need it most."

"A commendable way to do business, and kudos to you for giving back, but…"

"No buts, Rory. You are not going to be the exception to the rule."

"I'm not comfortable with this…can I write a…"

"If you say check again, I'm going to be insulted and think you're not a good listener."

Rory slid her hands on her hips. "That is not true, and I find it hard to believe that you'd even suggest it." Spinning around, she marched into the kitchen and started putting away the leftovers.

Max listened to the clang and bang of dishes and knew that she wasn't happy with his heavy-handedness. Unfortunately, there wasn't much he could do since this wasn't an area where he compromised. Deciding to risk life and limb, he walked into the kitchen and grabbed a towel. When she ignored him, he picked up a dish and began drying it. "So, what do you like to do in your free time?"

Rory turned off the water and scowled. "I'm not done being mad about your imperious ways and need more time to polish the speech I'm formulating to put you in your place."

"My place is at your side."

"I was thinking it was under my high-heeled sandal."

Max let out a loud bark of amusement. "I didn't think we'd start sharing fantasies quite yet, but hey, if you wanna walk down that road, then I'm all for it."

Rory threw a damp sponge at him and laughed. "Good Lord, this has been a day. My life is going up in flames, I have an alpha standing in my house telling me how it's going to be, and a stalker that thinks harming is the best idea since salted caramel sauce."

Max dropped the towel and ran his hand along her jaw. "I want to make it better for you…"

"I'm not used to having someone like you in my…"

"Corner?" he finished.

"Yes! I have my Mama and sisters, of course, but not an elite warrior who is willing to take on the bad guys."

"Guess it will be fun figuring out how we can both get comfortable with the new reality."

"And what reality is that?"

"The one where you and I get to know one another and see if this crazy chemistry is the real thing."

"I can only take on one major life change at a time, so this whole romance thing is going to have to be put on the back burner for a while."

"Alright, if you say so."

Rory leaned back and skimmed her eyes over his face slowly. "You agreed to that too easily. What kind of devious plans are you cooking up?"

Max held up his hands in innocence. "Me? I would never devise a strategy that would make it impossible for you to not only fall for me but profess your undying fidelity." He gave her a solemn smile. "I'm pretty much an angel and never do anything that would land me on the wrong side of the commandments."

Rory moved closer. "That's too bad because if I ever were to consider this romance thing, then I'd need to break at least three just to make it worth my time."

"Did I say…wrong side? What I meant was…"

She pressed her finger against his lips. "Don't dig a hole you can't get yourself out of."

Max moved her finger and took the irresistible woman's mouth in a searing kiss. When she met him, stroke for aggressive stroke, he knew that his match had finally arrived.

CHAPTER FIVE

The following morning, Rory opened her front door and was greeted with a frowning bodyguard. "Good morning, sunshine."

Max kissed her cheek lightly and then walked in. "I regret letting you talk me into leaving last night."

"Because I interrupted our hot make-out session or something else?" She watched his enormous shoulders drop along with a pile of irritation and frustration. "I enjoyed our naughty kissing if that makes you feel better."

He let out a frustrated sigh and looked at the ceiling. "As much as I'd like to focus on that, I can't because I've got a scum-sucking son of bitch to find, and having no blood in my brain is going to make it more challenging than I would like."

"Fair enough. I'll make you a coffee, and then we can discuss all things treacherous."

Pulling her against his chest, he kissed her head. "Just know that the minute we're done with this stalking BS, all bets are off, and you and I will be exploring how best to make the other addicted."

Not able to resist the unchecked desire in his eyes, she moved closer and wiggled her hips. "I'll move that idea to the very top of my list and start formulating strategies at the first available moment."

Growling, he took her mouth in a wild kiss. "I can't wait until the time is right to see what that means."

"Now, I have no blood flow." She took several steps back. "You behave, Max. We have business to take care of."

"Pretty sure you're the one responsible, but no matter."

She ignored the comment and went into the kitchen and told herself that sometimes the thing you feared most is the very thing you have to take on. Max wasn't a man to take lightly, and she knew that whatever they came up with would be life-changing.

There were too many delectable pheromones flying around to think otherwise.

Once they were settled at the table, Rory studied the too-handsome man and wondered what she was missing. "Can I ask you a personal question?"

"Sure."

"I know this is none of my business, but how come you're single?"

Max arched an eyebrow. "Are you afraid that I'm a dud or a weirdo?"

"Kind of…since you're too good to be true."

"It hasn't been my focus. When I was active on the Teams, I didn't have the interest or time to pursue anything long-term. Then I started SAI and didn't have the mental bandwidth to give anyone more than a passing glance."

"And now?"

"I'm ready, Rory."

"For what exactly?"

"You. And whatever we make." He pushed his cup aside. "A woman like you doesn't come along but once, and I'm smart enough to make the most of the opportunity we've been given." He traced a ring on her middle finger. "I hate this stalker bullshit, but I am happy that it brought us into the same orbit."

"I guess that would be a silver lining to all this nonsense."

"Sure as hell would."

Feeling better than she had in ages, she covered Max's hand. "Okay, tell me what has you in a mood and how I can help."

"I met with the team earlier, and our little show yesterday had the effect I was hoping for."

"That should be good news."

"It is, but I should've been in residence last night." He shook his head. "It's a mistake that I won't be making twice."

"Are we going to become roommates?"

"Something like that."

Dark sparks of desire flared in Max's gaze, and she knew that them keeping things PG was going to be challenging and perhaps a little impossible. "Okay, fill me in on what has developed overnight."

"It's not going to be easy to hear, but I believe that intel is power, and I don't want you operating in the dark."

"I appreciate that and can more than handle whatever it is that you have to share."

"Hope so," he mumbled as he pulled out a tablet. "My years in the service taught me to see what was, no matter how unpalatable. Because not doing so can be fatal."

"Understood," she said quietly, wondering when she would become immune to threats against her person.

Max cleared his throat. "You received an e-mail last night that originated from a computer located at the corporate offices. Whoever has you in their sights wasn't too happy to hear or see you with a man and made their feelings clear in the e-mail."

Feeling blood rush from her brain, she leaned back. "Well, too bad for him; he can just suck it." She pulled her laptop over and opened her e-mail. As she read the offending missive, her heart rate sped up. "I want to purchase a gun today and would appreciate it if someone could show me how to use it." She started to shake with anger. "And after we're done buying firearms, I think we should go to my office and make out in the hallway. Let's push this person's buttons, so they come out of hiding. Enough of this cowering in the shadows business."

"I'll make out with you anywhere you want. But let's form an effective plan before we return to the offices and put on a show."

"And the gun?"

"We can go to the firing range today and start your training. It takes several days to get a license, and you need to become proficient before you start packing one in your purse."

She gave him an assessing look and decided he was being sincere. "All right. Is there anything else I need to know before I go to Bob's office and give my notice?"

"We have narrowed the suspect list down to three people. Derick discovered some interesting things about Jackson that don't add up, and we want to keep him on our radar, even though we don't believe he's the one responsible for the e-mails."

"What does that mean?"

"We're not sure yet."

Rory ran her finger over the keys of her computer. "I've always been uncomfortable around him but couldn't tell you specifically why. My creep-o-meter pings more often than not when I'm in his company but I have yet to come up with a concrete reason why. He's never formed any real attachments to people and is volatile and prone to fits of rage. All in all, a really fun guy to work with."

"I knew you were uncomfortable yesterday when we were in his office and wondered if he'd ever done anything overt."

"How could you tell? I thought that I was a better actor than that."

"You held my hand tightly and stood slightly behind me. Something that I have learned in our short acquaintance that is totally out of character."

"I had no idea that I was giving off such clear signals."

"It's not obvious to civilians. I have well-developed Spidey senses and read your body language."

"Clearly." Crossing her legs, she shook her head. "Tell me what you found out about Jackson. I always felt like he was up to something but could never figure out exactly what."

"Derick and Laird have been running their computers since yesterday, researching the business of the hotels and the names I gave them. They've taken a thorough look at Jackson, and his bank accounts don't add up. The initial research suggests that he has a separate business of some sort—something that has made him a lot of cash. It appears to be tied to suppliers for the hotels. My best guess is that he's laundering money for someone and taking a cut."

"That makes a lot of sense and would explain why he's always up in my business. He's probably worried that I'll mess up whatever cash stream he's created."

"I think his skimming is connected to your stalker but can't give you any facts to back up that theory."

Rory stared out the window. "I wonder how much Bob is aware of and why none of his people have discovered Jackson's larceny."

"Maybe they have and are biding their time."

"Maybe," she repeated before looking up. "When you say research, you mean hacking into files, right?"

"It's pretty much the same thing. We simply access the sites that will ensure we are discovering the facts."

"That's an interesting distinction and one I should remember if I ever want to use it as it relates to you." She got up, opened one of her drawers, and decided that the napkins needed to be folded properly. Nothing like a little organization to get one's heart beating normally. Taking special care to ensure the corners were lined up, she let out a contented sigh.

Max joined Rory and wrapped his hands around her waist. "When you're done with that drawer, can you come and sit down so we can make a plan for the day?"

"Sure, I just can't leave this drawer in disarray."

"Understood."

She turned in his arms. "I feel better when everything is put in the right place."

"I noticed that when you lined up my desk accessories yesterday."

Rory gave the man another gold star for not making fun of her compulsion and finished lining up the last napkin. "I'll call my mom and see what Bob's schedule is. Hopefully, we can meet today, and I can make my formal resignation."

"That sounds like a good plan."

She looked up. "What are you doing today?"

"I'm sticking with you."

"Don't you have an empire to run?" Stepping away, she tilted her head. "I've been fine so far and don't see a need to be glued at the hip."

"Did you read that e-mail all the way through? There are some clear threats implied. The guy left nothing to the imagination." He stepped into her personal space. "I will not be taking any chances when it comes to your safety."

"Fine," she pressed her finger into his chest, "but don't forget I want a gun."

"We can get the process started, but you're not getting one today." He returned to the table.

"We'll see about that," she said quietly as she closed the drawer. This victim nonsense had run its course, and she wouldn't be participating any longer. It was time to take her life back. With Max or without him, she was going to become a force to be reckoned with.

***

Max returned to his office after finishing a meeting in the conference room and admired the woman sitting on the couch. He didn't know what he'd done to deserve the blessing but was damn grateful, nonetheless.

He'd just signed on a new client that was going to be hugely profitable, and there was no doubt in his mind it was time to hire a COO. Lucky for him, he had a hell of a candidate a foot away. "Hi, Rory, I have returned as the conquering hero."

She stood and gave him a once over. "That sounds like something that would involve a kilt, which is very exciting."

"If that's your lady jam, let me hop on Amazon and see what I can have delivered by tomorrow."

"My goodness, how lucky am I?" She swayed back and forth. "A man who will not only vanquish my enemies but roleplay. You are the whole package, Max."

Groaning, he looked up at the ceiling. "You gotta warn me, woman. Those sexy comments of yours are blasting my brain cells faster than I can generate them."

Rory folded her hands. "Of course. What with your advanced age, I shouldn't take any risks."

Max growled and scooped Rory into his arms. "I can more than handle whatever you've got in mind. Don't worry."

"Good to know." She pecked his mouth and then retook her seat on the couch. "Tell me all about the big fish you landed."

"It's a corporate account that is big enough to push us into the big leagues. We officially have too much business and too few resources."

"That's exciting. I thought you all were already the deadliest sharks in the water."

"We are but have been considered a boutique security agency. Now, we're a big freaking monster."

Rory held out her hand. "Oh, Max, that's wonderful."

Collapsing on the couch, he took her outstretched hand. "How would you like to join us and become our COO?"

"Wait…what?"

"We need you to run the operations side of SAI."

"A lovely offer, but one I can't accept since I haven't officially quit my current job."

"That's semantics. You'll be free as soon as you speak with Bob."

"I'm not ready to commit to anything new." She pursed her lips. "I'll run an operational analysis and give you my suggestions, though."

"Are you saying no to my offer because you don't want to mix business and pleasure?" He watched her small finger trace one of the more prominent scars on his hand. "Because if it is, know that I'm not concerned. I think we can have both."

"One can rarely have both." She looked up. "My life is on fire, and until I'm reasonably confident that I have some control over the flames, I won't take on anything new."

"Fair enough." He kissed her cheek. "You can start as a consultant and…"

"See if it's a good fit," she finished resolutely.

"I know we're a fit and expect before too long that will become abundantly clear, and you'll have no choice but to hop on this speeding train and enjoy the ride."

"We'll see."

Taking the placation in stride, he crossed his leg over his knee. "How did the conversation go with your mom? Do you have a time set to meet with Bob?"

"Oh, my gosh, you're not going to believe this." Rory let out a breath. "Bob is selling the company! He was diagnosed with the beginning stages of Alzheimer's about six months ago and decided that he wants to live with as little stress as possible. The doctors feel he has many years before it becomes completely debilitating, but he doesn't want to waste the time he has. The sale is almost complete, and I'm betting that news is going to make Jackson lose his mind."

"Do you think he has a clue about the impending sale?"

"Mom said that Bob has kept the deal quiet because of a confidentiality clause in the sale. And between you and me, I think he doesn't trust his son with the information."

"Which means whatever dirty side deals he's running are about to come to a screeching halt."

"Exactly," Rory responded. "Things are about to get interesting; that's for darn sure."

"Cheese and crackers, Rory. You are not going to be out of my sight."

"I doubt that will be necessary for long." She patted his thigh. "Mom invited us for dinner tonight, so I can speak with Bob and let him know that I'm ready to leave."

"Sounds great; I'd love to meet your family."

"I hope you feel that way after Mom grills you. She's been crazy worried and needs to put you through your paces before she'll relax."

"I look forward to addressing her concerns." Tracing a pattern on her arm, he sifted through the new facts and tried to determine which one was going to have the most effect on their situation. His gut told him that Jackson was at the center of Rory's troubles but couldn't point to a hard fact that supported the hypothesis. All he had was a bunch of circumstantial evidence, and that, unfortunately, wasn't actionable.

A situation he abhorred.

Rory was right about things becoming more interesting, he just hoped it was the kind he'd eventually enjoy.

CHAPTER SIX

The following morning, Rory lay in Max's arms and decided to blame the earthquake for her lapse in judgment. Had the world not been rocking and rolling, she never would've crawled into her protector's bed and sought comfort.

A story she planned on sticking with.

What if it had been the big one? She would've been remiss if she hadn't sought the maximum comfort available with only hours to live.

And, boy, oh, boy, did Max Bishop offer the most delicious comfort she'd ever had. He was a master at fooling around, and she took every lesson he'd provided seriously. Running her hand over the massive muscles decorating his chest, she sighed. "I will apologize for my lack of manners in just a minute."

"Don't you dare," he replied with a growl.

"Does that mean you enjoyed my near panic attack and how I chose to assuage my fears?"

"Yes. One hundred percent." Slipping his hand inside her nightgown, he ran his finger over her breast and growled with satisfaction. "If we were going to meet our maker, then better we should have smiles on our faces."

"I completely agree." Moving closer, she told herself that seeking physical comfort was never wrong, and since the man offered so much of it, she knew it was her duty to enjoy every drop.

She bit back a laugh and thought about how close they'd gotten to consummating their relationship…or situationship…or fling-alationship.

She'd been ravenous in her exploration, and lucky for her, Max had shared her enthusiasm.

At one point, she hadn't been sure where he began, and she left off, which suggested that the time was coming to go all in or retreat fully. Since the latter wasn't an option, she silently made peace with the former.

Max levered himself up on his arms. "Are you ready, Rory?"

"For what?"

"Us."

She looked into his uncompromising gaze and guessed that any sleight of hand she attempted would fail. The time of reckoning had arrived, and if she didn't pull her metaphorical big girl panties up and face the music, she knew it would be the regret of a lifetime. "I suppose that seeing what happens wouldn't be the worst choice in the world."

"Might even be the best," he replied quietly.

Pressing his mouth to hers, she breathed through him as they both took the kiss deeper. The strap of her nightgown slipped off, and being the gentleman that he was, Max took full advantage. Her body reacted immediately to the man's entreaty, and she did the only thing possible and moaned her approval. His head dipped, and she wiggled closer when he slid his tongue over her nipple.

A perfect shudder racked her body. How did he know what to do? His lips played against her skin as though he'd been given the rule book and memorized it.

Touching, stretching, and reaching.

They did their best to hold onto one another. Closer to exploding than she'd ever been, she was surprised when he pulled away.

"Baby, I'm right on the edge; we have to slow this down."

Sucking in a breath, she tried to make sense of his words. "Are the orgasm police going to show up and tell us we can't have any?"

"God, I hope not!" Max pushed himself up and ran his hand over his face. "We have a full fucking day ahead of us, and I don't want the first time we make love to be rushed."

"Of course," she murmured as she adjusted her nightgown. Feeling some kind of way about the stop in play, she wondered if he wasn't that into it. Perhaps all his previous blabber about being interested meant nothing. Or worse, he'd seen how generous her curves were and decided he wasn't really interested.

Not all men found women with more padding than bones appealing.

She pushed herself up, shook out her hair, and told herself it was his loss. Better she discover his bias now. No need to allow the little spark of attraction to grow. "I'm going to get ready." Standing quickly, she gave him a saucy wave filled with confidence and headed toward the door.

"Are you mad?"

She stopped in the doorway. "Of course not."

"Any chance you'll look me in the eye and say that?"

Complying with his request, she lifted her gaze and made sure it was filled with breezy confidence. "I am a bit embarrassed, but certainly not angry." She waved her hand in the direction of the bed. "Let's just forget about this and…"

Max stood. "I'm not going to forget about one of the best nights of my life."

"I hardly think it…"

He ran his hand through his hair. "The fact that I haven't chewed through the chain that is keeping my good manners intact is a freaking miracle."

Seeing him stalk in her direction like a lion made her wonder how literal the chain chewing metaphor truly was. "Oh…well…I suppose…"

Max engulfed her in his arms. "If I'm fifty percent right about how well we fit, then forever isn't going to be long enough."

Allowing herself to take the comfort he was offering, she rested her face on his chest. "I was thinking a month would be more than enough."

"Well, Rory, you thought wrong. Last night should've confirmed that, and the fact that it hasn't makes me think that I'm going to be the one navigating the ship of our relationship."

Her head flew up, and just as she was about to blast him with a response, she noticed that he was doing everything not to laugh. "Poking the bear is never a good idea."

"It is if the bear made a story up in their head that is one hundred percent inaccurate."

"It was closer to sixty percent, but I get your point."

"Good because I could drown in my desire for you." He cradled her head, pressing a kiss to her hair. "Which is a hell of a thing, given my aquatic skills. I've swum near the Arctic Circle, and it was a lot easier than this."

"Anything worth having requires work."

"Believe me, honey, that's a concept I'm well acquainted with."

It was probably best to leave a comment like that alone because anything she added would only reflect poorly on her character. "I'll leave it at that and scoot off to my room and get my work lady look together."

"I like the soft, sexy lady I woke up to and hope it becomes a regular thing."

Rory stepped out of his embrace and turned toward her room. "You never know what's possible."

And she truly meant it because several days ago, she would've laughed in the face of anyone who suggested that she'd find someone as irresistible as Max.

***

Max drove away from the gun range and looked at his unhappy passenger. "Guessing that you didn't enjoy yourself."

"I was sure that I would love it, and it's so disappointing."

"What part, specifically?"

"I had hoped that I would've walked away with a feeling of power and control. But I didn't. It just felt loud and scary. Is that typical?"

"Guns may not be your thing. I thought, when you kept your eyes open, you did well."

"I think you're just being kind." She glanced over. "I'm going to keep at it, though, and will keep my eyes open the next time we go. For at least half of it."

"That's probably a good idea," he said with a laugh. "Having your eyes open will make all the difference."

"I think you're mocking me, and that imperious tone is not sitting well with me." She gave him a slow once over. "Perhaps if you hadn't had your hands on me, then I would've been a better shot. I didn't see any of the other teachers touching their students so intimately."

Max didn't think the truth was going to be his friend in the situation. Rory was a horrible shot, and more practice wasn't going to make it better. Not everyone was meant to handle a gun, and the beautiful woman sitting beside him was one of them. And not because she lacked the Y chromosome. It simply wasn't a natural talent that she possessed. If there were a country that needed to be taken over, there would be no better candidate. Need to mount an insurgency? Rory was your person. Want to update the federal tax code, Ms. Basso was the one they'd call. "Being good at everything is unfair, so don't spend too much time worrying about your armament skills."

"I…" the phone buzzed in her purse, "will have a perfect response right after I take this call."

"No doubt," he muttered. As he piloted them toward the office, he thought about the e-mail that she had received earlier. The change in Rory's routine had agitated the stalker, and he hoped it would provide enough motivation for some foolish behavior. The holding pattern they were in was unacceptable since he liked nothing less than waiting for a fight. He wanted to go to it and solve it quickly.

Rory ended the call and let out a long breath. "That was my mom and she shared some interesting information."

"Does it have anything to do with your stalker?"

"I'm not sure. Apparently, Jackson has battled drug addiction for years—a fact that I was completely unaware of. By the time I met him, he had his act together." She flipped her phone over. "Well, as much as a sociopath can have their act together."

"I'm assuming he's using again."

"You would be correct. Bob has him under surveillance because he's been hanging out with some questionable characters. He didn't want the business to be at risk if he wasn't able to stay clean."

"A lot of things are starting to make sense."

Rory turned. "I know."

"He's not just a spoiled narcissist who isn't able to feel remorse for his actions, but a drug addict who has turned to crime to feed his habit."

"It's like a tela novella," Rory commented. "All we're missing are a couple of dead bodies and ill-advised romantic liaisons."

"I'm sure they're out there, we just haven't discovered all the intel yet."

"And we may never since Bob had his assistant send out the announcement regarding my departure. I have several reports to put together for the new owners, and after they're complete, I'm free. And unemployed."

"Considering you have a COO offer on the table, I doubt that will last for long." Rory looked out the window, and he knew that she wasn't ready to respond. Something he understood but was incredibly frustrated by since he wanted nothing more than to have the incredible woman in his world. In whatever way she wanted.

Several hours later, Max sat in his office and heard Rory's phone ring. When she picked it up and frowned, he knew a move was about to be made. God willing, it would be one they could act on.

Rory answered the call. "Hello, Jackson. Yes, I'm sure that you're surprised. No, I didn't feel it necessary to give you a heads up. After all, it's not your name at the bottom of my check each week. Yes, I've considered the consequences. No, I'm not going to change my mind. Jackson, that's rude and uncalled for…"

Max snatched the phone and listened to the rest of Jackson's vitriol. "Now, Jackson, you know that's anatomically impossible. Yes, it's Max, and it's your lucky day, you dumb son of a bitch. Why is it your lucky day? Because we're not having this conversation in person. If you ever think of speaking to Rory that way again, I'm going to have to show why the myth about SEALs is true. No, I'm not kidding. Rory has nothing to do with you anymore, and I will not hesitate to make that clear in whatever way is necessary." He pulled the phone away from his ear and listened to a barrage of nonsense, and decided enough was enough. "Make a good choice, Jackson, or be ready to deal with the consequences." He ended the call. "Well, that was fun." He handed Rory her phone. "I think he got the message." Rocking back on his heels, he shook his head. "Unfortunately, we've got a lot of awkward holidays in our future because I don't think he's one to forgive and forget."

Rory flipped her hair over her shoulder. "I'm capable of fighting my own battles."

"I know, honey; it's just that…"

"I wanted to tell him off, and you took that away from me. Next time, let me have a shot at it before you come in and save the day."

Seeing her displeasure let him know that he'd made a major tactical error. "Okay, but it's not like I could have stood by and let some crazy fuc—I mean, asshole—speak that way to my girlfriend."

"Did I become your girlfriend before breakfast or after lunch today?" she asked with a frown. "I seemed to have missed an important conversation."

"I thought it happened this morning when we talked about taking our relationship further, and you know…"

"Fooling around doesn't mean we are bound in some way and…"

"It does with us," he said stubbornly. "And you ignoring that possibility is disappointing." Leaning down, he gently kissed her and pulled her into his arms. "I want everything with you."

Rory shook her head. "You are too much, Max."

"Always have been and always will be." He pressed their mouths together, and the moment things heated up, his office door popped open.

"Big brother, I had no idea this is what happened in your office."

Max ended the kiss and stared at his younger brother. "Sean, you have the same lousy timing you always did." He dropped his arm over Rory's shoulders. "Sweetheart, meet my brother."

Rory looked between the two. "My goodness, are you all good-looking? Or is it just the two of you?"

Max didn't care for the smile she was giving his brother and pulled her closer. "Sean, this is my girlfriend, Rory Basso."

"No way, man." Sean snorted. "Someone who looks like her is never going to be your girlfriend."

Understanding that it was a brother's job to give his sibling as much grief as he could, he accepted Sean's jab. "Miracles are around every corner."

Rory laughed. "Sean, you must be one of the younger brothers?"

Max snickered. "You got it, sweetheart. Sean had to follow behind me growing up and has never gotten over it."

Rory slipped away from Max. "It's nice to meet you, Sean. Come and give me a hug. It seems like we're going to become friends."

Sean accepted the hug, and Max noticed the look of surprise on his face. *Get used to it. We may be Special Forces, but she has a special force all on her own.* "How long are you in town, brother?"

"I've retired and am no longer with Delta," Sean stated flatly.

"That's a surprise," Max said quietly, knowing there was a whole lot they would need to unpack. "Do you want to join us here?"

"Yeah, I guess. Eventually."

"We have a lot of requests for stuff in the Middle East, and we've turned it down because none of the guys want to return to the sandbox. If you're interested, then you can start developing that business."

"Give me a little time to figure things out, and I'll let you know," Sean replied.

"Whatever you want, man. I'm happy to see you healthy and in one piece." He tugged his brother in for a hug and thumped him hard on the back.

"So, there are four of you?" Rory asked, stepping back.

"Yes. Sean has been with the Army for thirteen years with Delta. Brett is an Air Force pilot, and the youngest, Brandon, is a SEAL."

"Your poor mom! She's had to worry about each and every one of you for all these years. She must be a saint or a heavy drinker."

"She's a true steel magnolia—pretty on the outside and made of forged steel on the inside," Sean said with affection. "She's not someone you want to tangle with, and our dad would be the first person to tell you that."

"Just the type of woman I love," Rory said as she gathered her things. "I'm going to get out of your way and let you two catch up. I'll head over to Birdie's house and check on her. Mark went wheels up today, and she could use a friend and a bottle of wine."

"I'll drive you over; just give me a minute," Max replied as he walked back to his desk.

"No way. I'm fine on my own; you stay and catch up."

"How are you going to get there?" Max asked. "Your car is at the house."

"I'm going to drive your car since you can catch a ride with your brother."

Max turned to his brother. "Did you ever meet Mark?"

"I may have when you two were on a layover in Germany."

"Mark is engaged to Rory's best friend. That's how we met. Birdie was worried about her, and Mark suggested that she give me a call."

"Is this the small world of SEALs again?"

"It is," Max said with a chuckle. "Whatever you need is only one phone call away."

Rory adjusted her purse and held out her hand. "I'll take the keys."

Max handed them over. "The only reason I'm allowing this is because no one will look for you in my car. Also, I have a team at Birdie's house installing a security system. I'll track you until you arrive and then have one of the guys check in with me."

"That's very overprotective and slightly controlling. I'm going to let it go, for now, since you're trying to save me from a stalker." She kissed his cheek. "We may have to revisit it after you catch the guy."

Max gave her a kiss of his own and made sure it was one she'd remember.

"Jeez, guys, give me a break. I've been OCONUS for almost nine months," Sean said with a groan. "I don't need to see that."

Rory pulled back. "It was his fault. I'm completely innocent."

"Women like you have never been innocent," Sean quipped. "You're like a package of C4. We just have to make sure you don't detonate and blow us up."

"I have no idea what you just said, but if it's a compliment, I accept. If it's not, then I am going to remember that when it comes time to buy you a present."

Max watched her walk out of the office as though she was Queen Elizabeth, except with more dignity. "God damn."

"When are you going to marry her, brother? Because if you don't, then I may have to."

Max turned his attention to his brother. "I'm going to marry her as soon as I can talk her into it. I've only known her for four days, so I've got a bit of wood to chop."

"Get on it, bro, because you don't want a woman like that to slip through your fingers."

"I don't plan on it." Max stepped out of his office and watched Rory stride down the hall. He didn't like the idea of letting her go off by herself but knew that he didn't have a choice.

A situation he was likely going to become familiar with.

***

Jackson sat at his desk and tried to calm down; he felt like a panic attack was imminent. Things were starting to spiral out of control, and it was probably time to cut back on the blow.

Even though it was the last thing he wanted to do since he still had a couple of things to navigate. There had to be a way to deliver on his promises and stay off his father's radar until the sale of the hotel was complete.

Was Rory quitting going to complicate what he'd put in motion or make things easier? He had no idea, and that meant it was still necessary to monitor what she was doing and saying. For all he knew, she had it out for him and planned on screwing him any way she could.

Pushing himself to his feet, he decided to see what Gavin was able to pull off of her computer. There might be a clue as to what she was really up to. He strode into the IT office and noticed Gavin was the last one working—a fortunate turn of events since he didn't need anyone overhearing their conversation.

He took a moment to study the mad genius and accepted that he was one click off from the rest of the world. The man's reaction was never what he expected, and he hoped that he'd picked the right guy for the job.

"Hey, Gavin. How's it going?" The look of guilt was unmistakable, and he wondered how far he'd taken the assignment.

"Hey, Jackson. Why did you let Rory quit?"

"I didn't let her quit," he replied sourly. "I had no idea she was thinking of leaving. She gave her notice to my father, and I didn't know until I read the e-mail. It might have something to do with her new boyfriend. Who knows?"

"I can't believe you let it happen!" Gavin drummed his fingers and rocked from side to side. "You were supposed to make sure she stayed."

Jackson rolled his eyes; the guy wasn't making any sense. "Why do you say that?"

"Because she must stay here. She isn't supposed to leave."

"Well, I can't do anything about it now. Her last day is next week."

"You need to do something."

He ignored the comment and moved on to what was important. "What has she been doing on her computer lately? Anything new?"

"No. She's been working on reports for your dad. You know how she loves her organizational charts and supply chain spreadsheets. Nothing unusual. There's something wrong with the camera, though. It doesn't work anymore."

"Why are you looking at her camera? That was never part of it."

"I did that on my own because I wanted to get as much information as I could...for you."

"I never said anything about the camera. What have you been looking at?" Gavin looked distinctly uncomfortable but defiant at the same time.

"I just make sure that she is where she says she is."

"Shit, Gavin. Don't look at her. If she finds out, that's grounds to press charges. You can't hijack a camera and get away with it."

Gavin sat up abruptly. "What you're doing is illegal. You have that side business going. Why do you always act like you're innocent and none of the rules apply to you?"

"I do what I have to do," he sniped back. "This is all part of the plan to keep the hotels profitable. It's fine."

"Does your dad know about it?"

Jackson felt a surge of rage. "None of your damn business. Don't do anything else. She's going to turn in her laptop next week, and I don't want to take any heat if someone finds out what you've done."

"It's not me. You were the one who asked me to do it. It's all you."

Jackson took a step toward Gavin and pulled him up out of his chair. "Scrub the goddamn computer."

Gavin pushed him off. "Get control of yourself. How much blow did you have today?"

"None of your damn business." Jackson wiped his mouth with the back of his hand. "I'm under control."

Gavin shook his head. "Is her new boyfriend a former SEAL?"

"Apparently. He's retired now and owns a business."

"I saw them kissing out in front of the building the other day. She shouldn't be doing that. It's not right."

"Rory can kiss whoever she wants. The guy is the real deal."

"No, she can't kiss whoever she wants. Do you think everything they say about those guys is true?"

"You mean about SEALs? Yeah, they are elite warriors. I can't believe she chose him."

"Maybe she had no choice. Perhaps he made her."

"I don't imagine so." He started walking out and stopped at the door. "Do what I told you to do. Because if I go down, so do you."

Jackson stalked back to his office and slammed the door. He was so close to finalizing his plan, and it was starting to fall apart. He needed a little pick me up, and then he could come up with an idea that would save the whole thing. Rory was not going to take this away from him.

CHAPTER SEVEN

Rory pulled in front of Birdie's flower shop and was startled when she heard the car phone ring. Pushing the button, she answered hesitantly. "Hello, this is Max's car, Rory speaking."

"Baby, why are you stopped? You're not at Birdie's house yet."

"How do you know that I'm stopped? Wait, don't tell me because I will just get mad. For your information, I'm picking Birdie up from the shop, and then we're going to get something for dinner."

"I'm going to have one of the guys come down and stay with you until you're ready to go to the house. The only way I agreed to this was if you were going from point A to point B. No stopping in between."

"I don't care for your tone, Max."

"That's too bad since all I'm trying to do is keep you safe." He gusted a sigh through the phone. "Honey, if I don't have eyes on you, I get real uncomfortable."

"God forbid you should be uncomfortable. What about me?"

"Rory, please don't bust my balls. I just want to keep you safe."

"Why didn't you just say that? Why do you have to be so controlling?"

"Said the pot to the kettle. One of my guys is going to come down and stay with you until you go to Birdie's house."

"Fine."

"When you say fine, you don't actually mean fine…right? This is some kind of secret language that I don't know about."

"Pretty much. Live and learn, Max. Live and learn." She disconnected the call and walked into Birdie's shop. "I'm here, and we are drinking martinis tonight."

Birdie walked toward the door with a vase in her hand. "From your mouth to God's ears. What kind are we going to make?" She set down the vase and hugged her friend.

They held hands just like when they were in second grade. Not much had changed except they drank martinis and ate sushi instead of Oreos and milk. "Max is sending someone over to keep an eye on us until we get to your house. He's paranoid and overprotective, and it's starting to bug me."

"Unfortunately, I have no words of solace because that's how they're made. The good comes with the annoying. The idea of someone being after you is probably making him crazy. If he could put you in a bubble to protect you, he probably would. I know Mark certainly would if he thought he could get away with it."

"I'm beginning to understand that. I appreciate what Max and his team are doing, but it's overwhelming. I went from complete freedom to none at all." She glanced around the shop and noticed how good it looked. "Can I do anything to help clean up before we go?"

"No, I'm done. Let's go home and make martinis." The bells above the door jingled as a big block of a man strode in. "Hi, Chris, we're almost ready to go." She watched him cross his arms as he stepped close to the wall. He was as wide as he was tall and always wore an expression that promised trouble for anyone who crossed him. "Chris, are you going to have a martini with us tonight?"

"No, ma'am. I'm on duty."

"When do you get off?"

"When the boss says so."

"Okay, maybe next time."

He nodded as if it was a possibility, which they both knew wasn't true. "It's you and me, Birdie." She flipped Chris the keys and smiled. "We're going to walk. Would you mind taking Max's truck back to Birdie's house?"

"I'll follow behind you and meet you there."

And darn it, the man was true to his word and drove slowly behind Rory and Birdie as they strolled home. Once they arrived, Rory gave him a wave and walked into the house. "I bet he'd like any other assignment than following me around."

"What's that?" Derick asked as he walked up.

Rory smiled at Max's partner. "Chris would probably prefer to be in a firefight than hanging out with me."

"If anything happens to you on his watch, his life is pretty much over," Derick commented. "And since you two look like you're up to no good, he'd probably much prefer to be up to his neck in tangos."

"I like to dance too, so I can see why he'd choose that over babysitting."

Derick gave her a pained smile. "Tangos are combatants."

"Are those the ones we don't like?" Rory asked.

"Yes. They are the ones we'd like to see…"

"How many men are here?" Birdie asked in a rush as she joined them. "I'm ordering food and want to have enough."

"Five," Derick replied succinctly.

"I'll triple my order and plan for fifteen."

"Good idea."

"I'm going upstairs to change," Rory commented before she left Birdie and Derick. She had an extra set of clothes in the guestroom and was ready to get comfortable and enjoy some much-needed girl time. Well, as much as something like that was possible with five large men in the house.

Thirty minutes later, Rory was settled in her friend's backyard under the sycamore tree. She handed a martini to Birdie and then took one for herself. "Tell me how you're doing."

Birdie shook out her hair. "I'm holding it together. I had a feeling that Mark was going to be called up this week and was somewhat prepared for the dreaded call. I know he loves his job and think he might've missed being in the middle of the action."

"That didn't answer my question. Are you ready to deal with his deployment?"

"I don't have a choice, Rory." She took a healthy sip of her drink. "I fell in love and gave him my heart. Whatever comes is what I have to deal with. Good or bad. He's, my person."

Rory took Birdie's hand and squeezed. "Whatever you need, I'm here."

"You've told me that since we were eight or nine, and it still makes me feel better."

"Good." They'd been best friends for over twenty years, and sometimes, the best medicine was just sitting together.

"So, tell me about Max. Have you fallen for him yet?"

Rory pressed her lips together and hoped that it would ensure that the truth wouldn't escape. When she felt like bursting, she let out a gust of air. "I may have. Even though it's probably a perfect recipe for disaster."

"Why do you say that? He's a good man, and Mark truly respects him."

She sank into her chair and sipped her drink. "If I fall for him then I probably won't recover." She looked from side to side. "I might want to keep him and then where will I be?"

"Happy...contented?" Birdie said quietly.

"Relationships have never resulted in either of those words. I fall, and the men disappear. It's a story that I don't want to repeat. Even if Max is the most enticing, beguiling, and captivating male that I have ever come across." She refilled their glasses. "Did I say sexy? Because he's certainly that. Not that it matters. We'll probably have relations one or ten times, and then that will be that."

Birdie pushed herself up. "Did he suggest that as a possibility?"

"No, he's called me his girlfriend and future wife a couple of times."

"That makes more sense."

"Absolutely not!" Rory squawked.

"I think Max is a breed apart from the men you've dated in the past and could be a terrific candidate."

Rory shook her head. "I am all kinds of smitten with the man, but I know that if I allowed myself to fall for him, and he dumped me…I would never survive." Draining her glass, she looked around the yard. "I think a fling is my best option because that doesn't entail broken dreams, bravery, or any other nonsense that will have me weeping into my coffee for a month."

"I support whatever decision you make. But prepare yourself because if Max has set his sights on you, then he will not give up. Mark was relentless in his pursuit and was brave enough for both of us."

Rory stared into her drink and had a feeling that Max was taking a page from the same playbook. He had no hesitation about what they could become and what place he wanted in her life. After years of men playing the ambiguity card, she didn't hate his certainty. In fact, she adored it—a concept that frightened her to bits.

"Give Max a chance and open your heart to the possibilities."

"Okay, Matchmaker Birdie, slow your roll. I've seen that look in your eyes before, and I will not become the focus of your efforts." She waved her hand toward the house. "Pick one of those men over there; they need your help a lot more than I do."

Birdie smiled. "You're right. They could benefit from my superior skills, and I should get started on it right away." Waving her finger at Rory, she gave her a warning. "This doesn't get you off the hook, though. Think about what I said. Max could be your prince charming."

"If Prince Charming was overprotective and paranoid, then I might agree with you."

"He's a SEAL; that's how they're made. Mark, Max, and all the men from the Teams are elite warriors and have demonstrated their trustworthiness a million times over in their careers."

Rory knew she was right, but that didn't mean you had to marry one. "So what made you fall for Mark so quickly? I've never seen you decide that fast."

"He ran at me full speed, and I couldn't resist. He's a grown man who knows his mind and heart and what he wants."

"What do you mean?"

"I think people hesitate when they start dating and are constantly weighing their options, waiting to see if there's a better deal out there. Mark never waited, not for one second. I thought I was the interested one, but he was *more* interested. It felt like he'd been waiting for me to show up, and once I did, he wasn't going to let the opportunity pass."

"If they put their lives on the line every time they are deployed, then that behavior makes a lot of sense. They must appreciate the brevity of life because they know how precious it is."

Birdie tapped her nose. "Exactly."

"Are you ready for life with an alpha?"

"I hope so since I'm engaged." Birdie tilted her head. "I want every piece of him. His heart, soul, words, body, and thoughts. I don't know if one lifetime is going to be enough."

Rory pressed her hand to her chest. "I am so happy, and you deserve this love story."

"We all do." Birdie leaned forward. "All we have to do is open the door when it shows up."

Rory knew it was true, but not if she was capable because letting someone in was the bravest act of all.

***

Max and Sean walked into Birdie's house, and it was relatively quiet—the kind that made him nervous. Once they made it past the kitchen, the volume rose by about a hundred percent. They both stepped onto the patio, and Max let out a snort when he saw what kind of shenanigans Birdie and Rory had started.

Five of his best men were sitting at Birdie's table, eating and laughing as Birdie tried to talk them into letting her do some match-making. There was a huge piece of paper propped up with diagrams indicating potential matches. Rory was directing the proceedings from the head of the table and taking her charting duties seriously when she wasn't laughing hysterically.

Rory clapped her hands to gain everyone's attention. "We can all agree that there are two very real possibilities for David and Ed. I expect the rest of you to support them in their efforts to ask these ladies out. Let's move on to Chris." The whole table groaned. "This isn't an impossible task. I would think a bunch of SEALs wouldn't shy away from a challenge. But maybe I'm wrong."

Max watched Birdie and Rory consult, and then they began presenting their candidates to Chris. It was like seeing a demented version of a dating game. "Is this what happens when I'm not around?"

Chris popped up and moved away from the table. "Thank God you're here; it was about to get ugly." He waved to Rory and Birdie. "Thanks for dinner and all the entertainment. But there is somewhere that I have to be."

As he made a hasty exit, Birdie called out to him. "You can run, but you can't hide. I'm going to find you the perfect woman, and then I expect to be made the godmother of your first child."

The table erupted in laughter, and Rory stood up. "Gentlemen, this is no laughing matter. Birdie takes this quite seriously. She's been doing this with mixed success since we were in the sixth grade."

The table fell silent, and Max walked over to Rory. "Sweetheart, you have to give these guys a break. They're not used to dealing with women who are smarter and wilier than them."

Rory smiled sweetly. "You seem to be doing okay. My brain doesn't seem to intimidate you at all."

"That's because I always planned on marrying up." When she didn't respond with something snappy, he kissed her head. "Is there any food left?"

"Of course," Birdie replied. "I'll make you a plate and let the guys take a break before the next round."

"I'll make their plates and meet you inside." Rory gave Sean a nod. "We'll put you next in line for the dating game."

Sean threw up his hands. "No thanks, all good here. No need to set me up."

"But…"

Max laughed and knew his brother could benefit from having a woman in his life. He just wasn't sure if he was ready. Max watched the men clear the plates from the table and joined the effort while his match made him a plate of food.

Once he set the dishes next to the sink, he gave Birdie a grin. "So, how many matches did you make tonight?"

"I have two solid matches and a possible third. And I will find someone for Chris if it kills me."

Max didn't doubt for a second that she was going to be successful. "I think you should find someone for Sean. He needs a good woman in his life." His brother almost choked and then recovered enough to punch him in the arm.

"Leave me out of it. How did I get involved?"

Birdie studied Sean with a gleam in her eye. "So, Sean, tell me about yourself. I want to know everything."

Sean groaned. "Birdie, I'm not in the market for anyone. I just retired and…"

"There is no time like the present. Just think how much easier the transition will be if you have a terrific girl. I have over twelve hundred friends on Facebook, and I'm confident that I can make a great match."

Max turned to Rory. "Is she really that good?" Rory stared at her best friend with love in her eyes and shook her head. "Sean, it's not the worst idea in the world." His brother gave him a glare filled with the promise of retribution, and Max shrugged. Lucky for him, he never had to worry about the dating game again because he'd found the one and planned on showing how good a match he could be.

CHAPTER EIGHT

Rory walked into the house with Max hot on her heels and wondered if he was still interested in what they had started that morning. There was no reason to believe he'd changed his mind, but she'd seen men flip too many times to be wholly confident. "So…"

Max made sure the alarm was set and then took Rory's purse and put it on the table. "I want our bodies and hearts to become one."

Surprised by the intense tone he used to make the proclamation, she stepped back. "I wouldn't mind if we continued where we left off, and…"

"I want to breathe you in and bury myself so deep that we can't tell the difference between where you end and I begin."

That made her take a step nearer since being close to any part of Max's Adonis body was on the top of her list. "That sounds like a very good idea, and…"

"I want to bring you so much pleasure that your mind rests."

"No need to involve my mind."

"I want your heart to beat so hard in excitement that you think it may stop."

"That might make the twelve orgasms I plan on having a bit challenging."

"I want to spill my soul into your body."

"Oh, Max…do you mean half the things you say? Because…" Before she could finish, he pulled her close and crashed their mouths together. The moment their lips touched, she was lost. Her body pinged to painful life as desire roared down her spine.

Maybe the man was a prophet because their mouths mating made her heart feel like it was on the verge of exploding.

Maybe Birdie had been right and refusing men with enough tenacity to fill a ship simply wasn't possible. Max was the most formidable force she had ever come in contact with and considering her matrilineal ancestry, that was saying something.

"I want you," he hissed as his hand slid under her sweater.

Feeling his fingers graze her rib cage right before he cupped her breast sent a wash of liquid happiness over her nerves. "Same."

"Are you ready to…"

"Yes," she replied as his teeth scraped along her neck.

"Just know…that when you let go, I'll be there to catch you."

"I'm counting on it." Moving away from his too talented mouth, she grabbed his hand and moved down the hall.

It was time to see if the man lived up to her fantasies.

Once they were inside the bedroom, Max gently turned her around and unzipped her dress slowly. Telling her nerves and insecurity to take a hike, she tipped her head forward.

"So beautiful," he murmured before turning her back around.

Rory dropped her shoulder and let the dress slither down her body. Praying that he liked what he

saw, she stood before him in a pale pink silk slip.
"I…"

"Jeezus, you are the most beautiful woman I
have ever seen." He lifted his hand. "I will try to go
slow but can make no guarantees." He skimmed his
fingers across her skin. "I can't decide where I want
to start."

The desire in Max's eyes was unmistakable, and
she let it silence every one of her doubtful thoughts.
He made her feel beautiful and wanted in a way that
she'd never experienced before.

Placing a hand on his face, she ran her fingers
over his skin. "My turn." She slid her hands up his
chest and made quick work of the buttons. When she
had freed him of the shirt, she let out a sigh. "You're
magnificent." Gliding her hands over his massive
chest, she enjoyed the feeling of his crisp hair under
her fingers. "I wonder what you taste like?" Leaning
forward, she ran her mouth over his chest.
"Irresistible."

"Not half as much as you." Moving closer, he
slid the strap of her slip off her shoulder and grinned
when it fell to the ground. "Lucky, lucky me."

She watched his gaze devour her as his eyes
scraped over her full hips and round breasts. Not
comfortable with his scrutiny, she moved closer.
"You have too many clothes on."

Max tore his eyes away. "I can take care of that."

His clothes flew off as he worked the zippers and
divested himself of the garments that separated them.
When he was naked, he stood before her with a lion's
grin. "My head is about to blow off."

Laughing, she looked down at his impressive erection and knew there was something else that was in danger of exploding. "Clearly."

Max let out a growl and advanced, sweeping her down on the bed. "I hope you're ready."

"Me too." He freed her of her panties and bra and then pulled her beneath him, making his erection press into her stomach.

"I'm going to apologize in advance since I'm on a knife-edge. The next ten minutes aren't going to be an indication of what I'm capable of, but I will make it up to you."

Laughing, she took him in hand and guided his length to her entrance. "I'm ready for my wild ride, Max."

"Thank God." He lifted himself on his forearms and slid into her slowly.

The sound of pleasure he made matched her own. It had been far too long since she enjoyed a man's company, and she felt her body climb toward its release. When his hand slid between their bodies and he stroked her bud, she detonated. Riding the waves of release, she held tightly to the man who made it possible.

A second later, Max shouted his release. "Now, you're mine."

Collapsing against the bed, she let her eyes close as she enjoyed the pleasure singing through her body. Had she ever felt this good?

Max dropped down and pulled her into his arms. "We'll need to do that about fifty million more times."

"Whatever you say, honey." And weirdly, she kind of meant it, which might become problematic if they were just having a fling.

***

Max was under Rory's spell, and he had no desire to do anything to make that change. In fact, he might commit a couple of sins just to ensure it never did. Looking down at the contented woman in his arms gave him a bone-deep satisfaction, the likes of which he'd never known. "In about ten minutes, I'm going to run my mouth all over your body and figure out what makes you happy. Then I'm going to keep doing it until you can't stand to be away from me."

"I will do my best to stand it."

Hearing her laughter fill the room made his heart trip over itself. Had he found the one? It sure as hell felt like it. Not able to process exactly what that meant, he pulled her beneath him and devoured her mouth in a kiss. "I'm gonna take a little tour of your body and see what makes you scream."

Rory waved her hand. "Do what you must."

"Plan on it," he muttered as he strung a string of kisses along her soft skin. When he hit the juncture of her legs, he inhaled her scent. Diving into her heat, he rubbed her sweet honey over his mouth. Rory's body reacted immediately to the attention. "That's it, sweetheart. Give in and show me how good I make you feel." He pushed two fingers into her tight channel and rubbed her sweet spot as he continued to devour her.

The grip of her hand in his hair told him she was close, and he doubled down and sucked her clit until she came on his mouth. Her sweetness coated his fingers, and he decided to rub it on her beautiful breasts so he could taste her sweet juices when he buried himself deep inside her heat. "Again," he commanded as he moved above her and pushed her knees up. Looking down, he felt himself lengthen. He lined up his cock and thrust home. He was grateful for the birth control patch Rory wore because it allowed him to go bare-back, a pleasure he'd never allowed himself. "You feel so good."

"More, Max. Give me more."

"Gladly." He leaned down and sucked her nipple into his mouth and tasted the sweet juice he'd put there. "Hold on."

He thrust hard and felt her contract. Smacking sounds bounced around them as he worked his cock in and out. Rory stilled and then yelled his name as she milked his body with hers. Her release triggered his, and he thrust hard one final time, feeling her body suck his seed right out of him. Feeling the world recede, he collapsed and knew without a shadow of a doubt that he'd found the woman he'd risk everything for.

An hour later, Max sat in bed with Rory with two empty ice cream bowls sitting between them. "To our last first time. It all gets better from here."

"I don't know if I could survive *better* since I'm almost positive that I lost several IQ points."

"Well, it's a good thing that you have a couple to spare." He picked up the empty bowls and put them on the nightstand. "We've refueled, and I'm ready for round three when you are."

"I don't have round three in me."

"Really?"

"Yes." She let out a long sigh. "I've not been in an intimate relationship for over two years."

"How the hell is that possible?"

"It's not that hard, actually. Once you turn it off, it becomes sort of normal."

"Why would you want to turn it off?" Max asked incredulously.

"Do you really want to know, or are you asking rhetorically?"

"I'm asking why you closed the door to romance, love, and sex. You seem like a person who would want all of that in your life." He pulled her into his arms and knew there was some asshole out there who had done a number on her. "Who in the hell broke your heart?"

Rory rested her head against the pillow. "It wasn't some huge heartbreak that caused me to take a break. It was a lot of small skirmishes that I lost. Somewhere along the way, I discovered that love might not be for me."

"But it could be with the right person."

"Anything is possible. One just has to have the intestinal fortitude to go after it, and I'm fairly confident that I don't possess that anymore."

"Is there any chance of you explaining how you arrived at this dark view of love? Who did you dirty, Rory?"

"Do we have to do this now?" She ran her hand over his leg. "We just had amazing sex, and I'd like to bask in the afterglow and not expose my soft underbelly."

"I want to know you."

"Why?"

"Because you feel like the one. And I'm guessing you might feel that way too since you decided to break a two-year hiatus with me."

Turning, Rory pushed her hands together. "I didn't experience some huge dramatic heartbreak; I just found the business of dating disheartening. More often than not, I misinterpreted the signals men sent out and falsely believed that when they said something, they meant it for more than five minutes." She shook her head. "I had a string of men ditch me right after I fell for them. It was like they knew the exact moment that I became attached. I would resist for weeks or months, and then the second I decided to give in, they moved on. The more I tried to figure it out, the worse it became. I kept thinking that the next man would be different, but that was never true."

"I don't know if I want to kill every son of a bitch who ever hurt you or thank them. Because if any one of them had figured out how amazing you are, you wouldn't be available."

"I'm not sure what I'm available for, so let's take a wait-and-see approach."

"You can, but I'm going to stick with my all-in strategy." He placed a kiss on her head and then pulled them down, so they were face to face. "I'm in, Rory, and don't plan on ever getting out."

"That's a lovely sentiment, but one I'm not ready for."

"Understood."

Rory yawned and then covered her mouth. "Just know that if I do decide to fall in love, it will be with you."

Max hit the lights, and the room was plunged into darkness. "That's good news, honey." Hearing her breath even out let him know she had surrendered to sleep. Rory may think there was a decision involved about love, but he knew different. Because whatever was happening between them wasn't a choice. It was fate.

Which meant that he had to find a way to show her he could be trusted—a monumental task he planned to achieve in the near future.

CHAPTER NINE

Rory sat in Max's office the following day and sent off the last report. She was officially done with a job that she spent six years toiling at, and she was relieved beyond measure. Her next move was still undetermined, but that didn't make her feel any less happy…in fact, it gave her a little shot of excitement. The world was open, and all she had to do was pick which direction she wanted to move in.

And the fact that Max strolled in thirty seconds later was not a sign from the universe. "Why are you frowning?"

"It's concentration, honey." He dropped into a chair and stretched out his legs. "I'm the happiest man in this whole damn building."

"Do you plan on telling me who or what is responsible for this jovial outlook?"

Leaning forward, he took her hand. "You are the source of my contentment and optimistic view of the future."

Heat flooded her body, and she attributed it to the memories of their early morning activities and not some sudden foolish desire to believe that he was the one and her future happiness was guaranteed. "Well…"

Max put his hand up. "Don't bother coming up with some fake argument. I know that you're fighting this thing with every ounce of your obstinacy and have no plans to give in to the sweet truth any time soon."

"I find that characterization of the situation…"

"Accurate?"

"No. It's filled with more holes than a piece of swiss cheese." Feeling his thumb trace her cheek made her realize that perhaps what he was saying had the tiniest thread of truth.

"Then, I suppose your surrender is just around the corner."

She wanted to wipe the smirk off his face and decided the only way to do it was with a kiss. Pressing her mouth against his made his declarations hard to deny. He took the kiss deeper, and she unfisted some of her fear. "I hope you don't turn out to be another lesson."

Max pressed their heads together. "I'm going to be the person who you count on most."

Rory nodded and then sat back. "Good enough."

"Are you ready for the updates on the asshole that's been harassing you?"

"Of course." Shifting her mind away from the conundrum of love, she straightened her shoulders. "Tell me everything."

"The team has it narrowed down to two computers and three possible suspects. Derick is running some deep dives in his cave of computers, and we should have something actionable within a day or two."

"It's hard to believe that this could be solved by next week."

"We've had some lucky breaks, and whoever is responsible seems to be getting impatient because they've gotten real sloppy over the last day or two."

"Thank you, Max. This news is giving me life."

"Isn't that what you said after I…"

She pressed her hands to his mouth. "We don't discuss that in the office." When she felt him smile beneath her fingers, she shook her head. "No more of your naughtiness."

"Until tonight," he said with a growl.

"Yes." Fanning her face, she instructed the pictures flying across her mind to disappear. "I'm done with my work for the hotels and am ready to offer my helping hands."

"Really? You are ready to become our COO?"

"No, but I will offer my organizational and operational guidance if you'd like it."

"Fair enough." He stretched his hands behind his head. "Why don't you work with Sean and set up the new division?"

"I'd be happy to." She pulled out her tablet and started a new note. "What should I know?"

"I'll set up a call with Rorke in our Virginia office. They've taken contracts for security in the Middle East, so he should be able to give you some direction. We've never taken any here because none of the guys wanted to return to the sandbox."

"The sandbox being the Middle East?"

"Yes, that's what we call it. Many of the men who are currently on the team have families and don't want to return. And the single guys have seen enough of it and are happy to stay in San Diego free of bullet holes."

"It makes sense. I wouldn't want a bullet flying in my body either." She looked out the large window. "Will I be stepping on anyone's toes? The last thing I want to do is usurp someone's place in line."

"We don't have anyone working that part of the business. Derick, Frank, and I play hot potato any time an org question comes up, and it would be great to hand it over to you."

"Alright. I'll dive in and see how best I can aid and abet the company's effort."

"Thank you." He let out a grunt of satisfaction. "Your first job will be to hire an accountant and payroll person. The person doing the job now is leaving us in a month because her baby is due at the end of December."

"I'm not a personnel expert, but I will see what I can come up with. Maybe Birdie has a recommendation."

"Sounds good and know that I trust you to choose the right person."

"That's the nicest thing you've ever said to me."

"The things I said earlier weren't as nice?"

"No, this is much better."

Max shrugged. "I don't understand, but I guess that's okay."

"Why haven't you hired someone before to help you run the day-to-day?"

"I have been playing catch up from the moment I opened the doors two years ago. We got slammed the first week, and it hasn't let up."

"Give me a topline of what the company offers."

"We provide corporate security analysis, which includes the physical location, people, and information management. It's a huge profit center for not only this office but the other six. We also recover people who have been kidnapped and offer personal security for executives and political figures. The Los Angeles office also does security for celebrities."

"Full service," she muttered as she thought about all the spinning plates the business must require. "Does each office operate independently?"

"Yes and no. We try to share resources, but the day-to-day decisions are left to the managing partner. When someone retires from the Teams, they are welcome to join us in whatever capacity they choose."

"This is an incredibly unique business. What's going to happen when you include people from other branches of the military?"

"That's an interesting question. I guess we'll have to wait and see. If Sean wants to add people that he knows, then I'm fine with that. I trust whatever decisions he makes."

"Because he's your brother or because of what he does?"

"Both. You do not become a Special Forces team member in any of the branches without possessing a unique personality and set of skills. Every person who has committed himself to that duty has put his life on the line and signed a check to the United States government with an amount of up to and/or including his life. That's a person who I want to work with. Full stop."

"How big do you see the business getting?"

"I've never thought about it. If someone wants to join us, then we find the right place for them. If we have the people, then we have the business. I haven't set a monetary goal but have set a human one, and I want any person who served this country to have a home here if they want it."

And if that wasn't the finest testament to his character, she didn't know what was. "Why do you think that I'm qualified for this? You need someone with more experience."

"You're the perfect person for the job. If you don't know how then hire someone to help you.

You've overseen the operations of ten hotels for five years. That involves a lot more moving parts than a security company. I trust you to make the right choice."

The faint sound of harps bounced around in her head, and she knew it was God's way of telling her that he'd delivered the very best candidate to make all of her dreams come true.

***

Later that afternoon, Max made their way down the beach with his brother and kept up an easy pace. They were going to do ten miles, and Max was looking forward to having the opportunity to find out why his brother left Delta.

After the first five miles, he figured it was time to dive in." "Do you feel like telling me why you left the Unit?"

Sean glanced over. "They wanted me to join the Black Ops team full time. If I'd done it, then a return home would never be possible."

"I'm guessing the decision was hard as hell and know that I'm proud of you for making the difficult choice. I promise to help you in any way I can."

Sean nodded. "Appreciate you, brother." He picked up the pace. "I've loved protecting my country, but the last several have been rough. Things are changing fast out there, and the lines are no longer clear. Our enemy today is our ally tomorrow. I don't have the stomach for it and don't want the only place I feel comfortable to be in some hell-hole in one of the Stans."

"If you stay out too long, that's all but guaranteed."

"I've eliminated all the tribal leaders I can and don't have the soul juice to keep playing the never-ending whack-a-mole game. I want to be able to function in the civilian world and relate to normal people."

"I'm glad you made the choice when you did because I would've hated to pull your ass out of the sandbox and drag you home."

"Let's just hope, I came home in time. I'm dealing with some pretty tough shit and know that I'm going to have to do some hard work to get on the other side of it."

"Let's get to it. I'll help you through whatever you need."

"Thanks, Max. I think this is something that I have to tackle on my own."

"I'm here and always will be. No getting rid of your big brother. Not in this lifetime or the next."

"Watch me," Sean said with a laugh as he took off at a fast clip.

Max followed him and loved that not much had changed since they were kids running wild in the backwoods around their house.

Once they made it back to Rory's house, Max noticed several cars. "What the hell?"

"When the cat is away," Sean said with a smirk. "Guess she got tired of your bossy ass already."

"Hardly, he mumbled as he pushed through the front door. Following the sound of voices, he strode into the kitchen and saw his two partners along with two women who resembled his beloved. "Are we late for the party?"

"No, honey. We're making pasta and will be eating in thirty minutes."

Max tipped his head toward Frank and Derick and then kissed Rory's head. "Guessing these two are your sisters."

"Guilty." A tall woman stepped forward. "I'm Catalina."

He received a slow once over and then a sharp nod. "It's nice to meet you."

"I hope you still feel that way after I put you through the Basso test."

"Never met a test I didn't like." A smaller and he hoped kinder woman stepped forward. "Are you Isabella?"

"Yes, and I will not be questioning you but will make a call if we find something we don't like."

"Fair enough."

Rory clapped her hands. "Enough. Let's have some wine and antipasti and catch up on gossip." She waved her hand toward the men. "Take the bottles and plates; we'll be out in a minute."

"We have our orders, men." He grabbed a plate and heard the women speaking in Italian as he and the guys walked out to the patio.

After Max had showered and changed, he returned to the patio and noticed Frank studying one of Rory's sisters. "You okay, man?"

"Yeah, just trying to gather intel. The women don't realize that I speak Italian and are divulging valuable tidbits right and left."

Derick shook his head. "It's not right."

"Yes, it is," Frank shot back. "Since they're debating Max's viability as a candidate for Rory."

Dropping into a chair, max grabbed a beer from the bucket. "Anything I need to act on?"

Frank smirked. "Apparently, you're a little pushy and overbearing."

"Tell me something I don't know."

Frank waved to the women in the kitchen. "You ever feel a connection so strong that it shifts everything you once thought you were sure of?"

Derick groaned. "Pretty sure you feel that at least once a week when you take a woman home from the bar."

Frank lifted his middle finger in a salute. "This is different."

Max shook his head. "Don't go after Rory's sister because the chances of it ending in a dumpster fire are too damn high. Not only will Rory be pissed and plot your demise, but Catalina will likely have you buried in the desert."

Frank began making a rebuttal but was cut off when the women brought platters of food to the table. Max gave him one last warning glare and hoped it was enough. He had enough barriers to tackle with Rory and didn't need the complication of Frank breaking Catalina's heart.

Max enjoyed the meal and wished his brother had stayed. He understood that the transition from active duty to retirement was rough, but he wanted Sean's company, nonetheless. Tuning back into the conversation, he listened to the sisters as they told entertaining stories about the various prom dates, they'd had over the years. Rory was laughing so hard that she had tears rolling down her face. Catalina was snorting as Isabella tried to finish describing the tux that some poor boy had worn when he'd come to pick up Rory.

"I didn't know that particular shade of blue was available in polyester." Catalina smiled at her sister. "Papa was horrified and didn't want Rory to leave the house with him. He felt like it would put a stain on our family name if she were seen in public with someone with such deplorable taste."

Frank leaned back. "Why was your father so upset?"

Catalina set her glass down and gave her attention to Frank. "Because Papa, along with his two brothers, owned a fabric mill in Sienna that imported wool used by some of the most renowned companies in the world. Clothes were important to them, and they believed that it said a lot about a person. And they didn't like what the powder-blue tux was saying about Rory's date. My uncles still own several shops that make bespoke suits that are coveted by some of the best-dressed men in the world."

Rory wiped her eyes. "The blue polyester tuxedo was offensive on so many levels that my poor father would've preferred that I miss the prom than be seen with the boy who wore horrible clothes."

Max ran his hand along Rory's arm. "That's why you're always so impeccably dressed. I've never seen someone with clothes that fit them so perfectly."

"Now, you know my secret," Rory replied with a wink. "Our uncles make sure that we all have beautiful clothes."

Catalina nodded her agreement. "My second-graders don't appreciate how well-dressed I am, but at least I know that Papa isn't rolling over in his grave."

The sisters were all quiet for a moment, and Frank leaned forward. "So, Catalina, where do you teach?"

"I teach second grade over at Her Lady of Sorrows Catholic School here in town. I taught first grade for the last several years but decided to make a change."

Max noticed that Frank's gaze had barely left Catalina's face since they'd sat down, and he'd bet good money the man was convinced that she was the answer to every question he ever had.

It was a feeling he had come to know and hoped for both of them that they somehow convinced the Basso women that they were their answer too.

CHAPTER TEN

A week later, Rory sat in Max's car as they drove toward the corporate headquarters of Bob's company. It was time to clean out her office, and she had a whole bag of mixed feelings. She was excited to move on to the next chapter of her life but wished the stalker thing had been resolved.

It had been deadly quiet over the last week, and she knew it was because all roads leading to her had been essentially cut off. Whoever had it in for was still out there, and she guessed they were simply biding their time. She twisted her hands together and reminded herself to be grateful that she had a super-sexy bodyguard to keep her company.

"Are you okay, honey?"

"Yes, I just wish all the loose ends were tied up."

"Agreed, and the longer it takes, the less control I'm likely to have when I meet the SOB face to face."

She gave him a faint smile and hoped it wasn't a literal statement. "Tell me what Derick and Frank thought about all the proposals I presented this morning."

"They loved every one." He glanced over. "You should know that I had to take some heat for not convincing you to join the company full time."

"I imagine you're well-acquainted with bearing a heavy load of responsibility, so I doubt it slowed you down for long."

"No doubt, but that doesn't mean I enjoyed having to explain my lack of sway with my girlfriend."

"Do I pull out the violin now or save it for later?"

Max rolled his eyes. "Love the sympathy, honey."

She ignored the comment and turned in her seat. "Did they sign off on expanding the warehouse and adding the gym and workout room? I think allowing the men to move their base of operations there is brilliant and will give you space to expand as new people are hired."

"They were on board with that and the daily delivery of cookies. They appreciated that you focused on what would help the operators and not the image of the company."

"Take care of your people, and they will take care of you."

"A theory that I've been putting in practice." Max folded Rory's hand into his. "I want to take care of you and will solve this stalker thing before you know it."

"I know." She squeezed his hand and had no doubt there was no one better in the world to have at her side. "Is there any news about Jackson? Has he made a last play at bilking the company out of more money?"

"Interestingly enough, the team just discovered a million-dollar deposit he made to a bank in the Caymans."

"What a fool." Another wave of relief washed over her, and she added being free of Jackson's company to the top of her happy list. "The fact that he commits such obvious larceny is a testament to how invincible he feels." She moved her gaze to the window. "What a shock it will be when it all comes crumbling down."

"Thankfully, you won't be anywhere near it."

"Amen to that."

Max turned into the parking lot and slid into a spot. "Tell me what's on the agenda today."

Rory dug through her purse and pulled out her small notebook. "I have to clear my office of all personal items, turn in my laptop and phone, and meet with HR. It might take several hours, so don't feel like you have to hang around."

"I'm not going anywhere." He looked up at the building. "We're eighty percent convinced that our person of interest works for the company, so I have no plans of leaving your side."

"So it's cheese and crackers today?"

"Every day," he mumbled as he pulled a pendant from his pocket. "I want you to wear this while we're in the building. Don't worry; it's not a real piece of jewelry. I see that look on your face."

"What *look*?"

"The look of horror at the possibility that I'm buying you jewelry. And ugly jewelry at that."

"Was I that obvious?"

"Yes, sweetheart." He slipped it over her head. "If we get separated, and you need me, pull the bottom piece out, and it will send an alarm to this receiver."

"Do you think this is necessary?"

"Not sure, but I prefer to be paranoid and safe."

"Alright, my Prince of Paranoia, I will wear your ugly accessory with pride."

"And I thank you, Queen of my heart."

Mushy feelings flowed with abandon, and in the spirit of change, she didn't try to fight them. Max Bishop's magic was working, and for the first time since she met him, she wasn't mad about it. "In a couple of hours, I'm going to be unemployed, so we should celebrate."

"I agree." He ran his thumb over his bottom lip and smiled. "Can we celebrate naked?"

"Why did I know you were going to say that?" she asked with a laugh.

"Because you had the same idea but didn't want to admit it."

"I was thinking of a martini and a nice dinner, but your idea has merit, too." Running her hand over his leg, she looked up. "I like you naked."

Groaning, he fisted his hands. "Don't say things like that when I can't do anything about it."

"Of course, no need to plant pictures of perfect debauchery in your mind just as we're about to be in the possible presence of my nemesis."

Max pushed the truck door open. "I'm ready to go in because, you're clearly not going to behave."

Watching him stride around the truck made a little party of butterflies takes flight. He really was the most delicious, heroic, and kind human she had ever encountered.

Two hours later, Rory stood in the elevator with Max and was happy to be one step closer to closing the chapter of her career at the hotels. The meeting with HR went better than she imagined, and she was excited that they had cashed out her shares in the company since it would provide a little nest egg for the future.

"Guessing you're happy with the results of the meeting."

"I'm over the moon. I am holding a big fat check from all my unused vacation days, and the first stop on my retirement tour will be the shoe department at Neiman Marcus."

"Congratulations, sweetheart." He dropped a kiss on her head. "Let me know when you go because I want to watch the master in action." Looking down, he whistled. "I like what you're wearing today. Those heels could be used as a weapon if need be."

"You're right." She lifted her foot. "I took a self-defense course, and the instructor told us to stomp on the assailant's foot, then knee them in the groin, and run like hell."

"Those are solid skills that every woman should know." The doors slid open, and they walked toward Rory's office. "Last stop."

"And the one that I like least since it's going to make me confront how much junk I've accumulated over the years." She stopped in the doorway of her office. "I forgot the bags in the truck; would you mind grabbing them?"

"Of course not." He lifted her pendant. "Don't forget."

"Wasn't planning on it." She watched him give her one last glance before he disappeared down the hall. Sighing, she looked at the stacks and decided that diving in was the only answer. Just as she was making some progress, she heard a shuffle of shoes and looked up, seeing the helpful guy from IT. "Hi, Gavin, how are you?"

"Not good, Rory."

"Well, that's unfortunate." She smiled and didn't know if inviting more conversation was wise. The man was as polite as could be but also creepy. He always stood too close, held her gaze for too long, and generally made her radar go off with alarms she couldn't explain. "I left my computer and phone with Rita in HR, and she said that she would send them to your office later."

"Why are you leaving, Rory?"

And so it begins. Why did the man always ask the most inappropriate personal questions? "It's time to move on since I don't have passion for the job anymore."

"Are you sure your new boyfriend isn't making you?"

Telling herself not to make a scene, she painted a patient smile on her face. "It's time to try something new." She looked down at a stack of folders and then lifted her eyes, feeling a sharp shiver run down her spine. Was this man her stalker? It would make sense if he was since he had access to all of her electronics.

Pulling in a calming breath, she tried to determine what her strategy should be. Should she grab her purse and make a run for it?

Was that too dramatic?

Considering he was blocking the door, it likely wasn't possible. She moved her hand to her purse and was glad that she'd picked up her gun yesterday. The pretty little armament was sitting in the bottom of her purse, and if she had to, she could use it. Even though she was a horrible shot and likely couldn't hit the broad side of a barn. "So…"

"You can't stop working here, Rory."

It is him.

The man was sweating like he was in a sauna, and his eyes were wild, darting from right to left. Perhaps she should lure him out of her small office. "I was thinking of going down to the lounge to get a soda. Do you want to join me?"

"No, no, I don't," he yelled. "You need to stop seeing that man. He's too big and mean. I want you to stop, Rory!"

Dread ran down her spine, and she knew that Gavin was more than one click off. He was clearly deranged. "I think you're saying those things out of concern, but I don't want you to worry. He is a good man and a war hero." Keeping the man engaged seemed like the best possible option until Max returned. "He protected this country for fifteen years while he was in the Navy." Seeing the flush of anger color Gavin's face told her she had taken the wrong tack.

"Quit saying that. He's not a good man, and you have to stop seeing him."

Before she could move away, Gavin grabbed her arm and tried to pull her out of the office. He was surprisingly strong for someone who worked at a computer all day. "Gavin, I don't want you to do anything that you're going to regret. I would like you to let go of my arm now!" Sweat trickled down her spine, and her heart sped up. Maybe the rush of adrenaline would help.

Gavin pulled out a big knife from the back of his pants and pushed it against her arm. "Shut up, Rory…shut up! I have to think. You have to come with me."

She attempted to jerk her arm from his grasp, and the knife sliced through her sleeve. Blood began running down her arm. Glancing down, she tried to remember if she had any vital arteries there. A wave of nausea hit, and she pulled her pendant. Gavin lunged toward her again, attempting to drag her out of the office. "Stop, my arm is bleeding! Let me get some tissues."

His face was bright red, and he sputtered viciously, "I hate that you made me hurt you. Why did you make me hurt you?"

Hearing those words ignited a match that lit the flame of her temper. She grabbed a wad of tissues, slapped them over her arm, and yanked her arm out of Gavin's hold. Furious wasn't a strong enough word to describe her emotional state. Two months of bullshit was enough! How dare he wave a knife around and blame her for what happened. She dug into her purse, grabbed the gun, and pointed it at the man who had been terrorizing her for more than sixty days. "You didn't expect that, did you?" She watched him back up and bump into the wall.

"You have bullied me for the last several months, and now you have the guts to come into my office and threaten me and slash me with a knife? I don't think so, you slimy son of a bitch."

She glanced down and tried to remember where the safety was. When she heard his feet move, she lifted the gun in his direction. "I think it's time that you get to experience a little of what I've been feeling since you decided to make my life hell." Waving the gun around, she let out a frustrated groan. "I'm not good with this thing, so I can't guarantee that I'm not going to hit something vital. But that's just the price you're going to have to pay." Sweeping her hair back, she prayed that her hero was steps away. "I'm normally not a violent person, but the last two months have changed that. Do you think this is how I wanted to spend my last day at the office? Well, I can assure you it's not!"

The sound of boots pounding down the hallway gave her the sweetest sense of relief she ever hoped to experience.

***

Max slid to a stop in the doorway of Rory's office with his gun drawn. When he saw the blood soaking the sleeve of his girlfriend's dress, he almost shot the man leaning against the wall on principal.

"Max, I would like you to meet my stalker, Gavin. I may want to shoot him. What do you think?"

Trying to get his heart rate to return to somewhere below the heart attack range, he let out a deep breath. "Well, sweetheart, if that's what you want, then I support you." He sucked in a long breath. "Just know that, if you don't, I probably will. But I won't take the satisfaction away from you. So if shooting the god-damn son of a bitch does that, I say go for it."

Gavin started to protest, and he watched Rory advance. Seemed his woman had hit her limit.

"Say anything, and I will shoot." She waved the gun around. "I am so mad, Max! He spied on me from my computer."

"You get to be as mad as you want, honey. No doubt about it."

Rory lifted her gun again and stared down the barrel. "I took the safety off, so I'm ready. I just haven't decided if I'm going to keep my eyes open."

Max wondered if she'd really take the shot or just needed to feel like it was possible. "Just remember that's it not that different from what we practiced at the gun range. Take a breath in, and as you let it out, squeeze the trigger. Remember, the shot is in between breaths."

Rory looked over and smiled. "Thank you, honey, that's good advice."

"Of course, I'm only here to help." He watched her hand shake. "You got this. I'm completely confident that you can make the shot. And if you miss, then I will finish the job."

She let the gun lower for a second. "That's the nicest thing that you've ever said to me. You totally remembered when I asked you to let me have a shot."

Accepting the praise, he realized that if anything ever happened to him, Rory was going to be fine. The woman had a warrior's bravery, and he couldn't have been prouder. "Even if you close your eyes, you're still going to hit something; just remember that."

"You can't shoot me. It's not legal," Gavin whined.

"What you did wasn't either," Rory said with deadly calm as she steadied the gun. "Just remember that if I make a lousy shot, my boyfriend is a SEAL, and he can make a kill shot from the next county. So, don't think you're getting out of this, even if I blow it."

He watched the color drain from Rory's face and knew she had only a couple more minutes left before she would collapse. "Honey, now would be a good time to take the shot. The police are going to be here in a second to take him into custody, and I don't want you to lose your chance."

Rory gave Gavin a disgusted look. "I guess that I won't shoot him since it will likely involve a lot of paperwork." She handed her gun to Max and then stomped over to Gavin. "I hope you get the help you need." She raised her foot, crushed it on his with her full force, and then kneed him in the groin. "Never piss off a woman in high heels since it's guaranteed to turn out badly."

Max slipped her gun into the waistband of his pants and watched the man crumple into a heap. He took Rory into his arms and kissed her head. "You handled that with a lot of grace and dignity."

The sound of police radios filled the hall, and he was grateful that the threat was finished. "Honey, let's get a paramedic to look at your arm."

"Okay. It's starting to burn, and I have a tight sensation in my arm. Also, I feel like throwing up."

Max led her past an SDPD officer who he'd worked with in the past. "Vern, I'll catch up with you after I get Rory some medical care."

"Sounds good." He hooked his thumb over his shoulder. "Paramedics should be down the hall."

"Roger that." Holding Rory tightly, he led her into the reception area and sat her on a couch. "Let's see how much damage that SOB did."

"Did I really just point a gun at Gavin?"

"You sure did, honey. And I'm damn proud of your courageousness."

"I wasn't really going to shoot him. I just wanted him to experience a little of what he put me through."

"I know." A paramedic joined them, and he tipped his head. A knife wound left arm."

"Got it." The paramedic examined Rory's arm. "He got you pretty good. Let's get the bleeding stopped."

Max noticed that Rory was starting to sway back and forth. "Hold onto my hand."

"Son of bitch," the paramedic grumbled. "It's too close to the artery, and she's losing blood fast."

Max slowed his breathing and flipped the switch in his brain to combat mode. No time for emotion or fear. The minute Rory's arm was bandaged, she fainted. "Shit." He scooped her into his arms and headed for the elevator. "Let's get her to the hospital."

Locking down the anger tripping across his body, he stared straight ahead and vowed to make sure that Gavin was locked away for a long time to come.

Many hours later, Max sat in a hospital room with Rory and held her hand. He knew that she was going to be fine but found the emotional turmoil overwhelming. How had he let the scumbag get close enough?

The doctor had explained that the injury, while bloody, wasn't life-threatening. Something Max understood intellectually but couldn't yet reconcile emotionally. "I'm sorry that I let him get near you."

Squeezing his hand, Rory shook her head. "You did no such thing. It was a hell of a last day of work, though. And as a reward for surviving the nasty business, I'm going to buy myself two pairs of shoes."

He laughed and kissed her. "I wanted to shoot him on sight but knew that you'd be mad since facing this head-on was important to you."

"And I appreciate it, Max. You've given me the best gift in the world: you gave me your faith and allowed me not to feel like a victim."

He had no idea how she came to that conclusion, but he wasn't going to argue with her. "I know you don't want to hear this, but I have to say it…I love you." Leaning his head against hers, he took a deep breath as her hand came up to his face.

"Oh, Max. How can you know?"

Before he could share the many reasons why he'd fallen, the door opened, and the Basso women entered in full force. They all spoke Italian at once, and he knew that giving them some room was his wisest choice, so he moved out of the way.

Catalina took Max's hand. "Thank you for taking care of Rory. I can't tell you how happy we are that it's over."

He wanted to tell her that he should've done a better job but felt it might not be the best time. "She should be released in the next couple of hours."

"I will take you to our house so that I can take of you properly!" Carolina announced firmly.

"No, Mama, you have enough to worry about with Bob. I want to go home and sleep in my bed. Max will be there to take care of me. He's a trained medic, so he knows what to do."

Carolina studied him for a moment before deciding whether he was qualified for the assignment. When he received a nod, he let out a grateful breath.

"Very well, then. I'll come by tomorrow and bring you soup and pasta."

"Mama, can you make me the almond cake? It's my favorite."

"Of course, *cara*, I would love to."

Max listened to the women talk for a while and was relieved to see that Rory was smiling. Maybe this wasn't the worst day in recorded history after all.

CHAPTER ELEVEN

The following morning, Max cracked one eye open and noticed it was still dark outside. Was the man responsible for threatening his woman really in jail? "Hell, yes," he murmured.

Wrapping Rory up a little tighter, he kissed her head and felt a slight wash of relief. Gavin was locked up tight in a cell, but Jackson wasn't, and until that situation was resolved, he wasn't going to let his guard down. As he ran several scenarios through his mind, he absentmindedly ran his hands over Rory's body and thought about ways to contain Jackson.

"I hope you're not trying to wake me up, Mr. Bishop. If you keep moving your hands like that, then I can't be held responsible for my behavior." Rory rolled over. "You smell yummy."

"Ms. Basso, if you stay like that, then I will be forced to give you a little morning loving."

"I dare you," she replied with a laugh.

Max had never met a dare he didn't love. He lifted her leg over his, tilted his hips, and slid inside the place he loved most. "How does that feel? Am I hitting just the right spot?" Using his massive leg muscles to get the leverage he needed, he continued his assault on her senses and her body. He thrust deep and hard and loved the gasp of pleasure his thick length provided.

"Like heaven, Max. You are perfection."

Moving in and out of her tight heat, he felt her tighten. Her breath caught, and he adjusted accordingly. "No place I'd rather be."

"Same."

He picked up the pace and knew that he was never going to get deep enough. He wanted his soul to be inside hers, and no matter how close he got, it never felt like enough. Short nails dug into his arm, signaling that she was close. Looking down, he watched as his woman came undone. A flush of color went up her neck as her climax rolled across her body. The sight of Rory lost in pleasure sparked his release, and he followed her over.

The last of the spasms left his body, and the feeling of her gentle breaths allowed him a moment of peace. For right now, they were exactly where they were supposed to be.

Rory kissed him gently and then flopped back. "Good morning to you. That was an amazing way to start the day."

"I aim to please."

"That you do." She dropped her hand onto his shoulder. "This is the first day of my new life, and I have no idea what to do."

"Freedom isn't always easy." He lifted her hand and pressed it against his chest. "I've loved living together. Any chance you want to keep shacking up while we date?"

Rory raised an eyebrow. "That's an unusual request."

"No doubt about it." He shifted closer. "You have woven a spell that I'm powerless to ignore. I'm addicted to your company and want to spend as much time together as possible."

"I want to get to know you outside of the crazy circumstances we've found ourselves in and see if…"

"You can fall in love with me the way that I have with you?" The moment the words were out of his mouth, he regretted them. Not the sentiment, of course, because he had fallen. But the timing.

They were not even twenty-four hours out from her attack, and the last thing he needed to heap on her already overflowing plate was his confession of love. "I know that this isn't the time to get into planning our happily ever after and apologize if my admission is poorly timed."

"Thank you." She grazed her hand over his jaw. "Giving into my feelings isn't easy, and it's going to take me a minute to get comfortable with the idea of knocking down my walls."

"No rush, Rory."

"Are you sure?"

"Absolutely. We have the rest of our lives to figure out what kind of kingdom we want to create." A smile lit up her face, and he decided that he'd done what he could to let her know which direction he was heading. And for now, that was going to have to be enough.

***

Several hours later, Rory drove toward Max's condo on Coronado Island and attempted to make sense of the jumble of emotions she was experiencing. The word that kept popping into her mind was unmoored—a completely unfamiliar place to inhabit since she was the very queen of processes, procedures, and structures.

Was she supposed to lean into this new existence or skitter back to what was comfortable and familiar? And because life wasn't topsy turvy enough, there was a man who seemed to think he loved her—a notion so foreign, she had no idea how to begin to unpack it. Or if she should. For all she knew, he was simply suffering from a case of terminal lust and would be over it by the time they hit the three-month mark.

Was that point of view pessimistic or realistic? Her experience told her it was the latter, even if Max was completely different from anyone she'd ever encountered.

He had no reason to sell her a false set of promises. There was nothing to gain from confessing one's feelings so freely. In fact, it was about the worst choice a person could make if they had an ounce of self-preservation.

Perhaps elite warriors didn't suffer from the same fear of vulnerability the rest of the population did. It seemed like a reasonable option since who in their right mind would choose one of the most difficult jobs on earth and believe it was their privilege to serve.

Round and round, her mind went with no neat answers in sight. Thankfully, she was saved from further rumination when the tall glass building where Max resided came into view.

Five minutes later, she walked toward the entrance with her bag slung over her shoulder and saw her super handsome boyfriend stride in her direction. "Hey, you." Before she could say more, Max swept her into his arms and kissed her like they'd been parted for days and not mere hours.

"Missed you," he growled against her mouth.

"I might've missed you a teeny tiny bit, too."

Max dropped her to her feet. "Don't get all gushy, woman. We wouldn't want people to think that you liked me or anything."

"My caution in expressing my feelings belies the very real connection we've made over the last several weeks." Looking up, she bit her bottom lip. "I may be slow on the uptake, but that doesn't mean that my feelings are any different than yours."

"Thank you, Rory."

"For what?"

"Giving me a tiny glimpse into your soul."

Raising herself, she pressed a kiss to his mouth. "Every relationship needs a tortoise and a hare, and lucky for us, we have just that."

"Lucky us," he repeated as they headed toward the elevator.

Once they arrived on Max's floor, Rory took a minute to look around. "I've never been in this building before. I like the sound of the ocean and the smell of the salt that wafts through those large windows."

"I never really got off the island after I came down for BUD/S. I loved Coronado from the moment I stepped onto the base, and when I left the Teams, I decided that I was going to stay put."

"Were you ready to retire?"

"No. I got banged up on an op and wasn't able to get cleared for active duty again. I have damage to one of my ears that prevents me from being able to dive. If you can't do that, then you can't be a SEAL. I also have a shoulder that was never going to allow me to make HALO jumps on any consistent basis."

"I'm sorry; that must have been incredibly difficult."

"It wasn't a lot of fun; that's for sure. But I was fortunate to have lasted as long as I did." He opened the door to his condo and beamed. "Welcome home, baby. Make yourself comfortable. I'm going to take this into our bedroom."

"Clever use of language...assume the sale, Mr. Bishop."

He winked and headed down the hall. "Take a look at the view. I'll be back in a second."

Following his instructions, she strolled out to the terrace. A view of the beach stretched out before her, with Hotel Del Coronado to the right.

Max joined her and dropped his arm over her shoulder. "What do you think?"

"I love it. You can see the people, but you can't really hear them. I love the sound of the crashing waves. You must sleep like a baby."

"I sleep best when I'm wrapped around you, and that could be anywhere."

She turned and smiled. "No need for flattery. I'm pretty much a done deal."

"You're never that, and I'm not fool enough to think otherwise."

The front door slammed, and she heard heavy footsteps.

"Quit kissing. I'm coming out," Sean called.

"Not possible," Max responded as his brother joined them. "How was the run?"

"Brutal and just what I needed."

"Are you going to dinner with us tonight?" Rory asked.

"No, I'm going out with some of the guys. David and Chris are showing me the local hotspots. Ed was going to join us but decided to go on the blind date Birdie set him up on."

"Brave," Max commented quietly.

"I'll have to call Birdie and let her know."

"That's right," Sean said as he wiped his face with a towel. "She flew to the East Coast when Mark was injured."

"It was touch and go for a week, and I know that she's grateful to be able to bring him home in one piece."

"Did you send the hotel's jet to collect them?" Sean asked.

"It's Bob's jet now. He purchased the plane for his personal use, and I feel fortunate that he was willing to put it at our disposal."

"Nothing more worthwhile than bringing a warrior home," Max commented.

"Couldn't agree more," Rory said, holding Max just a bit tighter. "According to Birdie, they'll be flying home tomorrow and bringing Travis with them. I guess he's in rough shape, and Birdie has decided that he needs to be under her care."

Max snorted. "I wish Mark and Travis luck."

"I didn't know SEALs needed luck since they are invincible."

"They are. Right up until they meet the woman who will change everything."

Max held her gaze, and she wondered if she was going to be the one who changed Max's life. It didn't seem possible, but who was she to predict the future?

***

Max sat across from Rory and wondered if he should give her an update. It didn't seem like the right time, and the last thing he wanted to do was spoil the happy mood. It could probably wait until tomorrow afternoon.

Rory tapped her nails against the table. "Are you going to tell me what's bothering you, or are you going to keep it in for a while longer?"

"It's nothing," Max replied with a smile. "We can talk about it later; let's enjoy our evening."

"Max Bishop, you better start talking and quit stalling."

"When you say my full name, it's not a good sign nor is the use of the word fine."

"Get on with it" She rolled her hand. "So we can move past it."

Knowing there was no way to distract her while they had their clothes on, he let out a sigh. "I'm going to preface this by saying that Gavin is still in lock up and not getting out any time soon. It looks like he'll be treated in a state mental health facility since he has a whole host of mental health issues that have gone untreated."

"What are you *not* telling me?"

"Jackson was the one who asked him to hack into your computer in the first place. Apparently, he wanted to keep an eye on you. At least that's what he told the detectives. According to my buddy, he concocted a big story about how he had concerns about the work you were doing."

"That is the biggest lie that has ever been told!"

Max covered her hand. "And there isn't a person who doesn't know it. Unfortunately, the SDPD doesn't have a way to prove it."

"I could spit nails; this is so infuriating."

"Which is why I wanted to save it until tomorrow."

Rory drained her drink and sat back. "More time wasn't going to make the information any easier to digest."

"Jackson didn't plan on Gavin's obsession when he asked him to hack into your computer, and his lawyer is trying to sell the detectives his innocence. No one believes it, but they have yet to acquire intel that will prove otherwise."

"The company isn't going to do anything about it either since the sale is pending, and Bob is in no shape to make his son take responsibility for his actions." Rory looked across the patio. "The best thing I can do is let it go because, if I don't, then it will eat me alive."

Max crossed his arms over his chest. "I fully support that but want you to know that the team is keeping tabs on his activities. We've shared the intel we've discovered with the DA's office, and if they can make a case, then justice might eventually be served."

"I won't hold my breath." Resting her face in her hands, she let out a sigh. "At least I'm not under threat anymore."

Max drained his drink. "I don't trust Jackson and consider him a threat. He's strung out and in business with the wrong people. That's a combination that can result in lethal mistakes. I want to keep you under protection until the sale goes through and Jackson either self-destructs or implodes."

"Alright, Max. I will go along with your plan for now." She gave him a stern look. "Just keep your overprotectiveness in check."

"Absolutely. Not a problem." And he silently vowed that it wouldn't be because the last thing he wanted to do was lose the race in the last mile.

"I doubt it's going to be that easy, but the sale is due to be complete in a couple of weeks, so we'll just keep doing what we have been."

He let out a big breath. "Okay, honey, that sounds great. Let's keep the status quo." Tension drained from his body, and he silently thanked his guardian angel for letting things work in his favor.

Rory's phone pinged, and she picked it up and read a message. "What the hell?"

He grabbed it and read the text. "God-damn son of a bitch! How did Jackson get your new number?"

"I have no idea." Rory picked up her water glass and drained it. "It looks like we're not going to have to wait long for him to lose his mind."

"I'm giving you a new phone on Monday with technology that will not allow this to happen anymore."

"Does it have magic powers to block assholes from texting you threatening messages?" Rory asked with a snort.

"Pretty much. I'll have Frank explain how it works since he's the one who's piloting the program." When she didn't debate the decision, he knew she was thrown by Jackson's latest bullshit. He fisted his hands under the table and prayed that he'd have a chance to confront the man at some point. No one threatened his family, and the sooner he could send that message to Jackson, the better.

CHAPTER TWELVE

You would think that getting rid of a stalker would all but guarantee happier times. That didn't seem to be the case for Rory. Did she have a super hot roommate who was a freaking genius in the bedroom? Absolutely. Was he well-mannered and considerate? Without a doubt. Was he on her last nerve because he redefined the words paranoid and caution? Hell to the absolute yeah!

But if he didn't want to find himself kicked to the curb, then he needed to check himself and take one or a hundred steps back.

Something, that wasn't likely given the fact they were currently engaged in their daily ritual of a staring contest. Neither of them was flinching, and she had no intention of giving in first. She'd learned that granting him an inch meant that he took a mile—a situation she didn't plan on allowing any time soon. "Max, you know that I can drive myself over to Birdie's house. Jackson isn't following me around."

"Why won't you let me drive you?" He lifted her hand and tried a smile that hadn't worked in a week. "Just think, you can read the news, or see if there are any good sales, or…"

"Find a nice private island that I can escape to, so I don't need to repeat this argument daily?"

"If you would just…"

"If you say cooperate, know that your friends will never find your body. I'm that mad."

"Seems a little dramatic," he mumbled quietly.

Rory leaned in. "What's that?"

"Nothing." He dropped her hand and looked at the ceiling. "Can I give my speech about my good intentions yet?"

"No. I have it burned in my brain and can recite it from memory."

Max let out a frustrated gust. "I don't have a choice about this without being an asshole, right?"

"Pretty much."

"All right."

Pretending not to be shocked by his agreement, she leaned up and kissed his cheek. "Good choice, Mr. Bishop."

"It's not like you gave me another one." He ran his hand through his hair. "What are you and Birdie going to do?"

"We're going to hang out and complain about the men in our lives." When his mouth formed a tight line, she took his hand. "We're both suffering from testosterone overload and need some talk therapy and a barrel of wine."

"Just a barrel? I figured you ladies were going to need a vat."

"One never knows." Looking down at his scarred hand reminded her that he was a warrior first, a man second, and her boyfriend third. He didn't know how to navigate the relationship business any better than she did, which meant digging up some patience would probably do them both a world of good. "Birdie is going crazy because Mark and Travis are lousy patients."

"That's what happens when you have two bored, aggressive, overgrown male children with too little to occupy their time," Max replied with a snort. "It's too bad that they can't have a van brawl and get it out of their systems."

"What in the world is a van brawl?"

"When we were in training, we would end up in a van for a couple of hours as we were being transported to wherever the next training exercise was happening. On a lot of those trips, a van brawl would erupt over something. Sometimes it was out of boredom, a stupid debate, or because someone spilled something. It's what happens when you have a bunch of guys with excessive testosterone pumping and no way to let it out. Every SEAL enjoys a physically crushing challenge, and if there isn't one readily available, we'll make up one."

Rory gave him a faint smile and wondered if there was any chance, she could tell her heart to stop loving him. It didn't seem likely because he was lodged in so deeply that excavating him would be damn near impossible. "You all are crazy, and I don't mean that endearingly."

"I understand, and that's why there are so few of us. We never miss a chance to compete. If we don't have something, give us five minutes, and we'll make something up. It's the nature of the guy who ends up on the Teams. I miss the hell out of it and would go back tomorrow if I wasn't so banged up."

Rory felt his loss on a visceral level and knew that she wanted his happiness above almost anything else. Except for her freedom. She wanted that more. "Does it ever go away…that longing?"

"It's always there." He shook his head. "That's why I started SAI. I wanted to recreate the Team experience and work with the men who had become my family."

"You have so much to be proud of, Max."

"I don't think of it that way. I'm just glad that I got to do my part."

It was a lot more than that, but she knew he didn't want the accolades for a job that he considered a privilege. "You are a good man, and I'm very lucky to be your girlfriend."

"Really?" he asked with surprise. "I had the impression that you were ten kinds of irritated and ready to dump me."

"I am frustrated and at the end of my rope most days, but that doesn't diminish my feelings for you."

Max embraced her tightly. "And what kind of feelings might those be?"

"Big ones, Max. The kind that are difficult to put words to and accept." When he remained silent, she looked up and was surprised that his eyes looked a little glassy. "You are hard to handle but so very easy to love."

Max closed his eyes and pressed their mouths together. "I'll see what I can do about the hard-to-handle part."

"I would appreciate that." She returned the kiss and hoped that her confession of feelings wasn't the beginning of the end.

***

Birdie opened the door with a big smile. "Thank God you're here. Those two knuckleheads are making me crazy."

"What are they doing now?" Rory asked as she crossed the threshold.

"They're bored and complaining about not being able to work out. They each have a week before they can start rehab, and I'm not sure we're going to survive."

"They need a project to occupy their time. Let's think of something they can do that won't require a visit to the hospital. Should I call Max and have him bring something over? We have a bunch of requests for security analysis for several manufacturing plants in Pakistan. They're at the bottom of the priority pile because he's short-staffed. That could keep them busy for a while."

"That's a good idea, Rory. Can you call him right now? I'm a little desperate," Birdie said with her hands clasped against her chest.

"Of course, maybe he can bring it by later this afternoon. What are they doing right now?"

"They're in the garage going through boxes and deciding what we should keep. Adam is starting on the update tomorrow, and I want to get rid of whatever we don't need."

"What are you doing with the garage?"

"One part of it is going to be Mark's man cave, and the other part will be a workshop and gym."

"Does he know about all of your plans?"

"Of course not. I wasn't expecting him to be home. It was all supposed to be a surprise. Adam is going to try and keep him off track as much as he can. Mark is going back to the base next week, so I have a small chance of pulling it off."

"Let me call Max to see if he can bring the packets by later."

"That would be great. I'm going to go check on the guys. It seems too quiet out there, and it worries me a little."

"Okay." Rory turned toward the French doors and saw Mark slowly walking toward the house and guessed the transition to civilian life wasn't going to be easy.

"Birdie, girl, we're going to Home Depot to get some racks for the garage," Mark called out. "Do you need anything else?"

Birdie strode toward the doors. "I didn't think you were supposed to be driving yet?"

"Travis is driving, and I'm going to be lifting. Between the two of us, we can get it done."

"I'm not..."

"It's happening," Mark said firmly.

Rory watched her best friend war with herself and knew it was taking every ounce of restraint not to argue further.

Birdie sighed. "Okay, what time are you guys going to be back?"

"Late this afternoon."

"Dinner will be ready at six, so be home by then, please."

"Yes, dear."

Birdie snorted. "You're getting good at that. I'm impressed."

Mark grabbed her hand and pulled her against his chest. "That was my intention since I want you to be impressed, the same way you were this morning."

Birdie glanced around. "You can't say that aloud. People will think that we're..."

Travis walked in and rolled his eyes. "Birdie, everyone already knows that you two act like rabbits.

It's not a secret." He shook his head. "Hell, half the neighborhood knows it."

"That's not true." Birdie turned toward Rory. "Is that true?"

"Probably."

Birdie stepped away from Mark and began sputtering. "That can't be…"

"We're going to leave before I get in trouble for lusting after my fiancée," Mark said with a laugh. "This is a no-win situation, so I'm going to Home Depot. Come on, Travis; let's make our escape."

Birdie shook her head. "I hope they make it there in one piece and don't hurt themselves when they try to lift stuff."

"They'll be fine," Rory said, taking her friend's hand. "Let's take advantage of the break and do something girly. Do you want to go to the movies?"

"We can watch one here if you want. That way, we can have margaritas."

"I like the way you think."

"Do you mind taking a walk with me first? There's an open house down the street, and I'm dying to see what the inside looks like."

"Of course not. You know I like to snoop and see what people do to their houses."

"Let's go and check it out. Maybe you can buy it, and then we can hang out all the time."

"How big is the house?"

"I'm not sure. Let's go look."

Ten minutes later, they were walking through the house, and Rory had never fallen in love so quickly. It was a shame it was so darn big. "If I had a family, this would be my dream home."

"It needs a lot of work, though," Birdie commented as she ran her hand over the banister.

"It's not that bad. The bones are good, and the kitchen is great. It just needs to be stripped of all the bad taste. Look…the floors have been redone, and the bathrooms are so charming. All the kitchen needs are new countertops; they did a good job with the rest."

"You're ready to move in. Are you sure it's too big?" Birdie asked hopefully.

"Uh…yeah…I don't think I need a two-story, five-bedroom home with a huge backyard for just me."

"What if you and Max get married? You could live here, and our kids could grow up together, and we could run in and out of each other's house whenever we wanted."

"You have it all planned out. Has Max been talking to you?"

"No. I just got home. Has he proposed?"

"No, of course not."

"Don't say it like it's an impossibility."

"It's not a probability."

"We'll see," Birdie said with a smile.

Rory walked toward the backyard. "Not every man proposes after a month."

"But some do," she said firmly as she joined Rory at the French doors. "Let me ask you this, if you never saw Max again, how would you feel?"

Rory felt a sharp pain near her heart and covered it with her hand. "I don't want to think about it."

"Then, make sure that whatever you choose reflects your hopes and not your fears."

Not able to respond, she squeezed Birdie's hand and followed her out of the house. Maybe it was time to leave the stories of failure in the past. Because whatever she and Max had didn't need to be polluted by what had gone before.

They deserved all the optimism she could muster and the belief that sometimes dreams really did come true.

When they returned to Birdie's house, Max was waiting at the gate. "Hi, handsome."

"Hey, beautiful." He kissed her cheek. "What are you ladies up to?"

"There was an open house down the street that we had to see," Birdie commented. "Rory loves it but thinks it's too big."

"Really?"

Rory took his hand and led him up the walkway. "It's a two-story, five-bedroom house with a big backyard."

"Interesting," he said quietly.

Rory glanced over her shoulder. "Are you in the market for some new real estate?"

"You never know," he replied with a wink.

Not wanting to dive into what the comment could mean, she followed Birdie toward the kitchen. Too big, indeed.

CHAPTER THIRTEEN

Max knew that he was traveling a road leading to nothing but trouble but couldn't for the life of him turn around. He was navigating unfamiliar terrain and didn't know where the damn map was so he could get himself out of the mess.

Two sides of him were warring, and he didn't know which one should take the lead. The warrior mentality that he'd honed for close to twenty years had always served him and the people under his command. He'd led men into battle and then brought them back out. And the only way he'd managed that was to be faster, smarter, better equipped, and a shit ton more aggressive. He was a sheepdog through and through and always had the safety of the herd at the forefront of his mind.

All good...right?

Not so much since Rory wasn't down with his *overprotective, annoyingly paranoid, and controlling ways.* Or something like that. There were a lot more unflattering adjectives that he had chosen to erase from his memory.

The love of his life had a damn impressive command of the English language and used it to her benefit and his detriment on an almost daily basis, and he didn't know if that should be considered a plus. He scratched his chin and decided to put it on the positive side of the spreadsheet since when they eventually had kids, it would benefit them.

Spinning his chair around, he looked out the enormous window that dominated his office and studied the San Diego skyline. Not that he had any kind of chance at making those kids since she was ten kinds of mad and about to kick his ass to the curb. He scraped his hand over his jaw and let out a low, frustrated groan. He was between a rock and a hard place. He knew that Jackson remained a threat, and that meant he wasn't letting his guard down any time soon.

His gut told him that more bad shit was headed their way, even if he couldn't prove it, which was the crux of the argument he and Rory liked to have at least twice a day. The darn woman wanted to flit all over town without a bodyguard, and he knew that was like rolling out the red carpet for trouble. He might as well put a billboard downtown announcing it was a free for all and anyone who wanted a piece of her could have it.

Dramatic overstatement?

Hell, no!

Jackson was up to his neck in some seriously dangerous crap, and nothing made a man more desperate than one who was playing with the cartels. Until the miscreant was locked up or buried in a shallow grave by his business associates, he didn't want to relax his guard.

Despite Rory's very loud protests.

The click-clack of heels sounded against the wood floors, and Max pushed himself out of his chair, preparing himself for the second skirmish of the day. "Hello, sweetheart."

Rory stopped just inside the door. "Why are you wearing that smile?" She took a step closer. "It's filled with guilt and a devious plan if I'm not mistaken."

Max walked around his desk and opened his arms. "I don't have any schemes cooking in my cauldron, so come and give me a kiss." Not one to be told what to do, Rory took small slow steps in his direction. "I'm as innocent as can be."

"That is a lie, and I bet if I called your mama, she'd tell me different."

Closing the last of the space that separated them, he engulfed her in a hug. "You liked my lack of innocence this morning."

Rory leaned back and lifted the corner of her mouth into a smile. "I do like that part of you… a great deal."

"We can lock that door, and I can show you some of the moves I've been saving up." Her body softened, and he had a moment's hope that she was considering the idea. But, of course, that didn't last long because she slowly pulled away from his embrace.

"As much as I'd love to fool around, I can't."

"Really?" He trailed his hand down her arm. "You've already done a ton for the company, maybe it's time to take the afternoon off."

Rory stepped back and bit back a smile. "That's exactly what I'm doing."

"Wait…I don't have that in my schedule. Where are we going?"

"To the day spa."

"Oh…"

"And in case you were wondering, I'm going by myself."

"No way, Rory." He watched her head fall forward as she let out a long breath. "The threat against you hasn't been resolved, and you need someone on your six."

"Max, I haven't worn a size six since seventh grade. I am a healthy size sixteen and considering how much time you've spent exploring my body, you should be well acquainted with that fact."

"What the hell are you talking about?" Grabbing at patience he didn't possess; he threw up his hands. "You need someone protecting your back. A bodyguard ensuring your safety so that Jackson and whatever criminal elements he's befriended don't think it's open season on my girlfriend."

"I can't abide this unrealistic view of yours anymore." Stomping her foot, she huffed out a breath. "You're coming dangerously close to crossing the line, and I don't find this behavior acceptable. You need to take a beat and decide if you want to push me further on this."

"I'm not taking a chance on your safety."

"I understand that somewhere in your head that statement makes sense, but the world outside of this office would not agree with that assessment."

"I doubt that."

"You have become a regular inhabitant of crazy town, and I can't join you there."

Not able to stop a smirk, he shook his head. "It's more like *make sure you don't come to harm* town, and I'm betting that a lot of people would like a slice of the pie I'm serving up."

"That doesn't make any sense."

"Agree to disagree." Grabbing his phone off the desk, he checked the calendar app. "I can clear my afternoon and join you. Heck, I need a haircut, so I might as well get it done today."

"You are not invited to my beauty day."

"What if I promise to be chill? You won't even know I'm there. I'll be like the wind."

"That might be true if you were out in the jungle chasing bad guys. But in a salon that specializes in waxing, not so much. Big men tend to stick out since it caters to a female clientele."

"That seems kind of sexist. Are men banned from the place?"

"Of course not." She tilted her head and tapped her finger against her mouth. "Actually, you can come with me—you just have to get something waxed."

"You're funny. I'm not getting anything waxed."

"If you want to come, then you can have some manscaping done."

"I'm not sure what you just said, and don't think that I want to find out."

"A big bad Navy SEAL is afraid of some hot wax? I find that hard to believe."

"I'm not afraid of hot wax. I just don't want it coming close to where I think you're talking about."

"I thought you had all kinds of experience in withstanding torture."

"I do, but that was in defense of my country. My country will be just fine if I don't experience hair being ripped from my body."

"That's unfortunate." She studied her nails. "My beauty day is planned, and it doesn't include your charming company. I'm going to the land of estrogen, and I'm not coming back until I have been buffed, scraped, waxed, and polished within an inch of my life. I'm going to read gossip magazines, eavesdrop on conversations, and talk about frivolous things while someone rubs my feet."

"I'll rub your feet."

"I know, honey, but I need to have a day away. We've spent over a month together, almost exclusively in one another's company. I need a break."

What could he say to that? Nothing that wouldn't have her running for the hills. Sucking in a breath, he nodded. "I don't want anything happening to you."

"I know, but if you don't want me to lose my mind, then you need to back off."

"Can I at least drive you over?"

"No, I'm going by myself. You have GPS installed on my car, and I know you put a tracker in my purse and have my phone linked up to your central system. You have eyes on me, and that will have to be enough."

"I don't like it, but realize that I don't have a choice."

Rory walked over and placed a sweet kiss on his mouth. "See, that wasn't so hard."

He squeezed her and then stepped back. "It's damn near impossible, but losing you is not on my list of things to accomplish today."

"Excellent." She stepped toward the door. "Don't send Chris to follow me, either. He has plenty of work to do here."

"Message received."

"I'll see you at home tonight. Dinner will be ready at seven."

"All right, call me if you need me."

"I will."

He walked to the door and watched her walk down the hall.

Rory stopped in front of Derick's office. "Max is going to come here in a second and ask you to track me with all the fancy gizmos that have been planted on me, my car, and my phone. I'm going for a day of beauty and wanted to give you a heads up and let you know my plans. If I get really crazy, I may stop at Whole Foods on the way home."

Derick crossed his arms. "You have a really good sense of humor about this."

"That's what I keep telling myself about a hundred times a day. I know he does it because he cares, but he's making me nuts."

"It's just the way we're wired. Any one of the guys would do the same thing."

"I told him he could come if he had some manscaping done, but he decided to pass."

"I don't know what that is, but it sounds painful," Derick said with a shudder.

"I know that you all are elite warriors and not afraid of anything on this planet. Yet when I put *hot wax* and your *man parts* in the same sentence, it seems to make you all a little nervous."

"Unless we're saving our country or a person, there is no way that we're going to let that happen willingly."

Rory turned and muttered under her breath, "Wimps."

"I heard that," Derick called out, "and that's not nice."

"But it's true."

Max watched her go out the front doors and tried to remain calm. It went against every instinct he had, and he didn't know if he would be able to stop himself from following her.

Derick stood in the doorway of his office. "Don't even think about it, man."

"I wasn't…"

"Yeah, you were, and I'd hate to see you blow your one chance at happiness."

"Me too," he mumbled as he returned to his office and dropped into his chair, praying that Jackson did something actionable soon. Because there was nothing he wanted more than to quit fighting with his woman.

They had a happy future to build, and that was going to be damn near impossible if they were fighting twice a day over her safety. He'd much rather love on her and make every one of her dreams come true.

Because her happiness had become his— something he didn't ever see changing.

CHAPTER FOURTEEN

Two weeks later, Rory sat in the airport and wondered if her heart rate would ever return to normal. It didn't seem possible since she was fairly confident that she'd just broken up with Max.

A concept that was causing her more pain than she could bear even if she didn't see another option.

She had asked him in every different way that she could think of to back off, and he couldn't make himself do it. Her independence was too precious to give up, and until Max could get himself under control, she needed to be free of his company.

An overwhelming sense of sadness enveloped her as a first tear slipped down her face. Why was she so emotional lately? Perhaps it was nothing more than a culmination of the months-long stress fest she'd been through. Or…no, it certainly couldn't be that. Wiping the idea from her mind, she shook her hair out and decided a chat with her best friend was in order.

Once she had her on the line, she felt better. "Birdie, do you have time?"

"Of course. Where are you? I hear a lot of noise."

"I'm sitting in the airport in Chicago."

"What are you doing in the middle of the country?"

"I had to get out of town before I harmed Max in a way that would be difficult to explain."

"And you decided Chicago was the perfect place to visit in winter?"

"No, of course not." She took a sip of her tea and hoped it would settle her stomach. "I am visiting all the SAI offices and evaluating the operations arm of the business. Once I'm done, I'll make recommendations and see if I can't increase their efficiency. I'm also assessing the feasibility of creating a corporation."

"Oh, that makes a lot more sense."

Rory smoothed out a wrinkle in her slacks. "I think that I broke up with Max."

"Wait, you're not sure?"

"Well… I told him not to call or track me down. I also said something about not wanting his paranoia near me ever again."

"I'm so sorry; what was the straw that broke the camel's back?"

Recalling the conversation made her blood boil. "He forbade me from going on this trip without him."

"He actually used that word?"

"Yes, those were his exact words. Needless to say, I lost my temper and told him where he could put his overprotectiveness."

"I'm assuming it wasn't someplace comfortable."

Feeling a bubble of hysterical laughter form, she studied the people milling about. "And you would be correct. It also wasn't anatomically possible, so there's that."

"What was your parting salvo in this war of words?"

Another tear slipped down her face, and she wiped it away quickly. "I don't want to see your face again if this is how you're going to behave."

"Yes, those are certainly break-up words. Except you used the word 'if.' That suggests a small window of opportunity."

"A very small window."

"Hold on a minute; I want to ask Mark a question."

Rory crossed her legs and heard her ask about something that explodes. Why was that important information to have? She leaned back in the chair and wished that she was tucked away in her cozy home and napping. She had been so tired lately.

"I'm back," Birdie announced. "I told Mark what was going on, and he said he'd have Max over so they can talk."

"I doubt that will be helpful."

"Maybe he can talk some sense into him."

"That's like asking inmates to help the other inmates. All they do is reaffirm the other's warped view of the world."

"That's a very pessimistic attitude."

"I know, and believe it or not, I'm embracing it."

"I'll ignore that for now. Anyway, the point that I wanted to make earlier is that Max may see a small opportunity as a big opportunity. That's how SEALs think. An opportunity is an opportunity, no matter the size. They like to use C4 to blow things up if they think it will create a bigger advantage."

"That's not making me feel better." She heard Mark's voice in the background and Birdie shouting something back.

"The man of my heart informed me that I wasn't using the C4 analogy correctly. I informed him that if he wanted any C4 action later on, then I was using it correctly."

"Did he agree?"

"Of course, he did." She sighed into the phone. "So, what do you want to do next?"

"Sleep."

"Perhaps you should take a long vacation and visit your family in Sienna for the holidays. Get out of town and see how you feel after a couple of weeks."

"I think that's a great idea. I could hide away with my great aunts and uncles, cook to my heart's content, and think about nothing of consequence."

"That sounds lovely. Just be home by the twenty-ninth, so you can attend our wedding on New Years Day."

"Alright." She drank the last of her tea. "Thank you for listening to me."

"Always," Birdie said firmly. "I know that Max loves you, but that doesn't mean it's the kind you need. And that's okay."

"I love him, Birdie." Tears fell from her eyes, and she cleared her throat. "But I know that doesn't always mean that we're meant to be together."

"You don't have to decide either way. Put it aside for now and give yourself a break."

"You're right." She stood and gathered her things. "I'm going to buy several gossip magazines and then find some ice cream and relax before my flight takes off. I'll also banish thoughts of Max Bishop for the foreseeable future."

"That's a perfect plan. Love you. Call me if you need me."

"I will. Love you, too. I'll keep you updated." Rory ended the call and resolved to let her questions about the future go. A little self-care was in order, and she planned on making it her focus and not the man who had saved her life and showed her what real love felt like.

***

Max walked up to Birdie and Mark's house and felt like it was his last hope. If anyone was going to influence Rory, it was going to be Birdie. He knocked on the door and waited; glancing down the street, he saw the house that he and Rory now owned. There had to be a fix, he just didn't know what it was.

A week had passed without him hearing her voice, and he was as close to losing his shit as he'd ever been. Why hadn't he been able to control himself? Just as he was about to knock again, he saw Mark slowly approach and open the door.

"Do you feel as bad as you look?"

"Probably worse."

"So, this has been a bad week for you?"

"The worst of my life," Max confirmed with a rough voice.

"Come in. Birdie will be back from the shop in a little while."

"Has she spoken with Rory?"

"Of course. They've chatted a couple of times. Unfortunately, they speak in Italian, so I have no idea what they're saying."

"They do that, so we won't know what they're saying. I hate that."

"Evidently, they've been doing it since they were in Junior High. I almost started worrying that they were talking about me until I remembered that you're the one in the doghouse."

"Enjoy it while you can," Max said as he followed Mark into the house.

"I plan on it because I'm sure my turn will come soon enough." He dropped into a leather club chair that faced the window. "Birdie is grateful that I'm alive, so I have another couple of weeks before my sins start catching up with me."

Max took the chair to Mark's left and rubbed his face. "What if she never gives me another chance?"

"You can't think like that," Mark admonished. "Pull your head out and start acting like a commander and come at it from another angle. Work the problem, brother, just like you did downrange. There's nothing that can't be solved, and that includes Rory."

"Evading a nest of tangos and extracting hostages and intel when the odds are not in your favor is a lot easier than getting Rory to forgive me." He shook his head. "I fucking made it through fifteen years of impossible and never felt this way."

"I suggest you relax and give her room to come back to you. Did you buy the house?"

"Yes, it closed yesterday. I put it in both our names and am planning on giving it to her for Christmas."

"Solid plan," Mark replied. "But you might want to hold off until Valentine's Day. If you give her a key to her dream house when you're not even dating, it might not be received well."

"Well aware of that."

"Give her the space she wants and then ask her out on a date with no pressure. She has to believe that you are capable of normal."

Max threw up his hands. "That's the problem! I'm not sure if I am." He leaned his head against the back of the chair. "I'm crazy in love, which makes me crazy overprotective. I want to wrap her up in a bubble and tell her what to do."

"You need to make sure that she never finds out what you just said."

"I know that." The front door creaked open, and Birdie walked in with a grocery bag. Pushing himself to his feet, he walked over and took the bag. "Thanks for having me over for dinner."

"I'm only doing this because I love my best friend and want her to be happy."

"I understand and appreciate a chance to fix what I broke."

"I'm going to get dinner started, and then I will return with some very clear instructions."

"She's really good at that," Mark commented with a smile. "And likes to include the details that make all the difference."

Birdie took Mark's outstretched hand. "You are not supposed to be talking like that with company over."

Max strode into the kitchen and felt the full weight of his failure. He wanted his woman back so he could show her how very important she was to his existence. The world was gray without Rory in his life, and if he had to jump through a thousand hoops, change his SOP, and learn how to dance, then he would. There wasn't a mountain he wouldn't climb to give her what she needed.

Birdie joined him in the kitchen and started unpacking the groceries. "Do you love her, Max?"

"With everything I am," he replied solemnly.

"That's what I thought and why I'm willing to help."

"I appreciate it."

She nodded and then pulled two beers out of the fridge. "Take this to Mark and talk to him, please."

"Did he get the formal notice?"

"He sure did, and I know it's going to be difficult for him to accept."

"I'll do what I can." He walked back to the living room and knew what Mark had in front of him. Transitioning from active duty to civilian life was damn hard. It had taken him a good long year before he had accepted that life on the Teams was over. Hopefully, Mark's transition would be easier, though how that was possible, he couldn't say.

Hell, he was still transitioning. Most days, he still acted like the commander he'd been and not the man he was trying to become.

Was he ever going to get it right?

CHAPTER FIFTEEN

Life wasn't getting easier, and Max didn't know how he'd survived the week. It had been absolute hell since he hated nothing more than sitting on his hands and doing nothing. Moving the contracts around on his desk, he tried to refocus on the business he'd been busting his ass to build.

Before he got halfway down the page, his mind was kind enough to produce a memory that featured his stupid, testosterone-driven compulsion to keep Rory safely tucked under his wing.

Speaking of that, he realized that his partner in the Florida office hadn't checked in yet. He'd been receiving daily reports from the guys as Rory visited the various offices. What the hell was Joel doing? The guy always had his shit wired tight, so if he had missed a call, then it meant something was up. He checked his watch and decided to give him another hour before he sounded the alarm bells.

Pressing his fist into his chest, he let out a long breath and knew if he could just hear her voice, the pain would recede. He felt like something was about to break inside. For a hardened warrior, that was a difficult concept to understand since he always thought only his bones could break and not his heart.

Hearing his phone ring, he shook off his malaise. He checked the display and let out a breath when he saw that it was his partner in the Florida office calling. "Hey, Joel. How is Rory?"

"I'm not sure, man, since I haven't seen her. She texted last night and said that she didn't need a ride from the airport and would check in later regarding dinner plans."

"And…" Max said with patience he didn't possess.

"I never heard from her. I figured she was tired from the traveling and didn't think much about it until this morning. I've been waiting at the office, and she has yet to show. Can you give me her hotel info so I can go check on her?"

Fury and worry warred, and he didn't know which one was going to win. "What the fuck? How could you let this happen?"

"I didn't let anything happen!"

He leaned forward and closed his eyes. "She's been following her itinerary closely. This doesn't make any sense."

"Guess she decided to go off the reservation."

"Shit." He pushed himself out of his chair and strode down the hall. "Give me ten minutes, and I'll have everything sent to your phone."

"Roger that. I'll be on standby." Joel cleared his throat. "Maybe she's just tired and is taking a day off. Rorke called yesterday to let me know that she was at the airport and said she seemed a little tired and never really ate anything. Maybe she caught a bug and is just resting up in the hotel."

"Let's hope so because I can't let anything happen to her."

"Understood."

"That's my future wife and the source of everything good and right in the world." When Joel didn't respond, he realized that not everyone was interested in his marital plans.

"I got your back," Joel said quietly. "Just get me some intel, and I'll be out the door in five minutes."

"Stay frosty; it's coming your way." Max slammed into Derick's office. "She's missing."

"What the hell?" Derick said as he spun toward his keyboard.

"Rory isn't following her itinerary. I just got a call from Joel, and she was a no-show."

Derick's hand flew across his keyboard. "On it. Give me a couple of minutes."

Max pulled his phone out and dialed Rory's mom. He needed to ask her for a big ass favor and see if they'd loan him the jet so he could get his ass to Florida by the end of the day.

Derick worked his computer and pulled up the info on Rory's tracking devices in her purse and briefcase. "She's in the Miami area, but the signal is faint. If there is too much cell activity, it will slow down our ability to pinpoint her location. I knew we should've upgraded to the new software."

Max ended his call with Rory's mom. "The jet is going to be ready in an hour. I can be in Florida by tonight. I'm going to grab my go-bag and head out. I'll have the sat-phone, so I expect immediate updates. Let's treat this as a snatch and grab until we have further information. Send everything to Joel; he's ready to leave his office as soon as you get the intel."

Frank strode in. "Is this for real?"

"Sure as shit is," Max bit out.

"Do you want us to run facial recognition on the security cameras in the airport?"

"It's running right now," Derick said. "Unfortunately, it takes a while. I don't want to hack into the Federal database unless we absolutely have to."

"It's gonna be in about ten minutes if we can nail her location." Max ran back to his office and grabbed his bag and gun. Tucking it into his waistband, he stopped at Derick's door. "I'll give you my ETA once I speak with the pilots."

"Roger that," Derick replied.

Frank slapped him on the shoulder. "We got this. It's just a blip. It'll be straightened out before you know it."

"Yes, it will," Max said as he headed for the door. Because there was no force strong enough to take Rory away from him.

When he was airborne, he received an update from Frank and Derick. Apparently, she was at the Eden Roc Hotel, not where her initial reservation was booked. She also used her personal credit card and not the corporate one.

Something was up, and he was going to fucking figure it out. He'd left a message on her cell phone, and of course, she hadn't returned his call. The advice that Birdie gave him was running through his mind as he sat in his chair. He was definitely going to use it when he saw Rory.

It had taken Derick longer than he would have liked to get Rory's room number, but they had it, and Joel was en route. Before too long, he'd have an answer.

Telling himself that he had a lot to be grateful for, he focused on the facts. Rory hadn't used her credit card at any other locations. She had checked into the hotel, and by all accounts, hadn't left.

His sat-phone rang, and he quickly answered, "Hey, Joel, please give me some good news. I'm about two hours from landing in Miami."

"I'm not sure what kind of news I have for you."

"Just spit it out."

"I know the security guy at the hotel, so I was able to confirm that it was Rory who checked in. I reviewed the security footage, and it was definitely her. I went up to the room and listened, and all I could hear was moaning. I'm not sure what kind of moaning, though. I checked the security cameras in the hallway, and it doesn't appear that anyone went into her room. She has the 'Do Not Disturb' block on her phone and hasn't ordered room service or anything. My guy doesn't want me to go into her room unless we're sure she's in danger."

"It's not what you think."

"I'm not *thinking* anything, man. Let me know what you want me to do."

"I want you to sit there until I arrive and update me if anything changes. I'll see you in a couple of hours."

"You got it. See you when I see you."

Max sat in his seat and became still. He analyzed all the information he had and knew in his heart that Rory wasn't with another man. She was probably sick and needed him to take care of her.

It didn't matter what she'd said before she left. They were going to be together, and that was that. He took a deep breath and switched to combat mode: quiet breathing, clear thought, and swift action.

***

Max stood in front of his friend in the hallway. "Anything new?"

"No, a little bit of moaning and maybe crying. It's been quiet for a while."

"Thanks, man; I can't tell you how much I appreciate this."

"It was nothing. Hell, you saved my life when we were on that op in Somalia. You want me to hang out for back-up?"

"No, thanks, I'll call you tomorrow. You can tell the team that we're clear and let them know that I'll call them later to thank them." They shook hands, and he turned toward the door and let out a big breath. He needed to prepare himself mentally for whatever he was going to see.

He knocked lightly on the door before he slipped his key card in the door and entered. Calling out her name, he waited for her to respond. The last thing he wanted to do was frighten her, so he moved slowly. The sliding doors were open, and he could smell the ocean and something else. Standing next to the bed, he let out a huge sigh of relief when he saw the woman of his dreams asleep. The bathroom door was open, and he noticed her clothes on the bathroom floor, which was strange because she was as tidy a person as he'd ever met. Stepping into the bathroom, he finally realized that Rory had been throwing up and must be sicker than a dog. Poor thing. And he wasn't there to make sure she was okay.

Returning to the bed, he studied her closely and noticed how pale she looked. How had this happened? He walked back to the bathroom, gathered her clothes, and put them in a plastic bag for dry-cleaning.

Looking around the room, he located her purse and dug for her phone. Once he checked it, he realized it was dead, something she had never let happen when they were living together. What the hell had happened? He looked through her purse for more clues and found a box of crackers and a big bag of sour gummy worms. As far as he knew, she never ate candy. Something was clearly going on, and he knew he'd have to wait until morning to find out what.

Pulling out his phone, he texted the team a sit-rep so they wouldn't worry and knew his decision to fly across the country was a good one. Rory needed him, whether she knew it or not.

He got out of his clothes and called her name as he lay down next to her. As his body hit the mattress, she rolled into him and mumbled something. He wrapped her up in his arms and breathed her in. The world righted itself as far as he was concerned, and for the first time in too many weeks to count, his heart beat slowed down. "It's okay, sweetheart. I got you. You're okay."

"Max, too early...not time to wake up."

He kissed her head. "Sleep, baby."

"Mmmmhhhmm."

Her head fell against his chest, her hand moved to his waist, and his world clicked into place. He hadn't slept much since she'd left and decided he could give in to the exhaustion.

All he ever needed was Rory in his arms. And right now, he had just that.

CHAPTER SIXTEEN

Rory woke up against a hard surface and didn't know where she was for a moment. They were not at home, and she was sleeping in a robe. She tried to lift herself, but Max had his arm securely around her, anchoring her against his chest. She smelled the ocean but knew they were not at his condo. She was in Miami, in a hotel and her boyfriend was snoring. "Max, wake up."

His eyes flew open. "What happened?"

Feeling sick to her stomach, she pushed away and ran to the bathroom. "Not again."

Praying to the porcelain goddess, she was barely aware of Max's presence until she felt him pull her hair up.

"I'm here, baby. I got you."

She waved in between bouts. "I don't want you to see me this way."

"Too late, sweetheart. I'm not leaving."

Before she could say more, a second round started. Was there anything worse than losing your cookies in front of your boyfriend?

Five long minutes later, she decided the monster that had taken over her body was done torturing her. A bottle of water was pushed into her hands, and she managed to take two sips. A wet washcloth appeared, and Max wiped her face gently. "Am I dead?"

"No, honey. You're gloriously alive and well."

Not understanding the comment, she raised her gaze. "What are you talking about?"

"I'll explain it after you've eaten something."

Rory waved her hand. "Uuugh. All I want is sour gummy worms."

"You have to eat something, honey."

Narrowing her gaze, she remembered that they were not together. "What are you doing here?"

"When you didn't make your meeting with Joel, I got a heads up and flew out to make sure that you were okay."

Feeling dizzy, she leaned against the cool tile. "I'm so disoriented…"

Max pushed himself to his feet. "I'm going to call a doctor. How long have you been throwing up?"

"I don't know, maybe two weeks." She picked up the wet cloth and ran it over her face. "It's my new morning routine, and I'm not enjoying it. I don't know where I caught the bug, but it hit me hard when I got off the plane in Miami. The smell of jet fuel had me losing my crackers in the bathroom at the airport."

"Why did you change hotels? You were booked at the Marriott."

"I wanted to smell the ocean and remembered how much I loved this hotel when I came here with my family."

"Makes sense."

"No, it doesn't." She leaned against the wall and wondered if he going to pick up where he left off and annoy her with his overprotectiveness. "Max…"

He put his hands up. "I'm reformed and was simply curious."

"I doubt that," she mumbled.

"Do you want some ginger ale or Seven-Up?"

"I don't know if I can keep it down. What day is it?"

"It's Friday."

"What day did I get here?"

"You're plane touched down in Miami on Thursday at one am."

Ignoring his meticulous knowledge of her every move, she shook her head. "Wow, I must've truly been sick. I remember throwing up and then sleeping. I've been really tired lately." Not able to refuse his outstretched hand, she took it and got to her feet, making the mistake of looking in the mirror. "Oh, dear…I look so…"

"Beautiful," Max finished as he wrapped his hands around her waist.

Wiggling away, she flapped her hands. "I have to get cleaned up."

"Rory…"

She leaned against the counter and shook her head. "Give me a few minutes."

"Okay." He kissed her head. "I'll get a doctor's appointment and order some food."

"Pancakes," she said quietly. "Please."

"Of course."

She watched him reluctantly leave and told herself that she wasn't going to fall into his arms until they came to an understanding. The man needed to accept where the hard lines were drawn and respect them. Otherwise, she was going to do the impossible and extract him from her heart.

And then have to discover how to live a dull life void of color.

Thirty minutes later, she was as put together as possible and decided that it was time to deal with what she and Max could or couldn't make. She walked out of the bathroom and felt her breath catch when she saw him sitting in a chair next to the patio.

There wasn't a better-looking man in the whole universe. A streak of jumbly nerves crisscrossed her chest, and she decided to welcome it instead of pretending like it didn't exist. "Is breakfast coming soon?"

Max popped to his feet. "Should be here any time." He opened his arms. "Any chance of a hug?"

"I suppose." She walked into his embrace and told herself not to cry. There was nothing she loved more than being in his arms.

"I love you, Rory, and am sorry that I went so crazy before you left."

"I..."

He pulled away and cupped her face. "If you say that you're finished..."

"Don't interrupt."

"Sorry."

"I love you, but..."

"You do?"

"Yes, you infuriating man."

Max scooped her into his arms and held her tightly. "You have made me happier than I deserve."

When he set her down, she shook her head. "I may love you, but that is not some free pass. We're going to have rules...codes of conduct...parameters...and..."

"Rules of engagement?"

"Yes, I like that one. We're definitely going to have that." She heard a knock on the door. "We'll discuss this after breakfast."

"I'd love nothing more," he replied before answering the door.

Once she made it through half the stack of pancakes, she pushed the plate away. "Those were delicious."

"Why don't you have a little more?"

"I don't want to tempt fate." Max covered her hand. "You look very relaxed."

"I am…now that we're…"

"Together?"

"Yeah." He ran his finger over her hand. "When did you decide that you love me?"

"I think it happened a while ago." She lifted her cup and sipped her tea slowly. "I didn't want to give into it, though." She looked up. "You are such a force of nature, Max, and I didn't want to get swallowed up by you and your ideas of how this thing between us was supposed to go."

"I know that I can be a lot to handle, and I never meant to make you feel railroaded." He hitched his shoulder. "I've never fallen in love before and am not sure how to handle the power you have over me."

"I don't have any…"

He put his hand up. "You do. You're in my heart, soul, and mind. I want you next to me for all the days to come, and the idea that it might not be possible guts me in an indescribable way."

"Wow, I had no idea."

"Now, you do." He looked down at the table. "I want to make a life together."

Sometimes, the best choice was the one that held the most risk, and she knew that the man sitting across from her was worth going out on a limb for. "After we agree about what that could look like, I am willing to try."

"I look forward to our negotiations."

She folded her hands together. "As do I."

"Maybe I should love you up before we start." He moved closer. "So all my finer qualities are fresh in your mind."

"I guess it couldn't hurt."

"Might even help."

Ignoring the need his hungry eyes created, she cleared her throat. "The most important thing I need is for you to move down the scale from bat-shit crazy to slightly overcautious."

"I will do my best, but don't want you to think that I'm suddenly going to ignore all my instincts."

"I understand that what I see is what I get. Probably, as you get older, it's only going to get worse. All I'm asking is that you moderate it and hover to the right of sane."

"I can probably do that."

"See that you do." She waved toward his plate. "Now, finish, so we can have some very naughty make-up sex."

"Done," he replied with a laugh as he jumped up and pulled her toward the bed.

Laughing, she fell under him and decided that loving the man was the best investment she could make.

***

Max kissed Rory with the full force of his feelings and slipped his tongue inside her mouth. She tasted perfect. When he inhaled her scent, he realized that it had gotten inside of him and was now as much a part of him as his own beating heart.

The urge to consume her and absorb every ounce of her in every way possible was stronger than anything he'd ever felt. "Is this too much?"

"No, it's just right," she replied against his mouth as she opened her legs.

Pressing kisses to her face and neck calmed him just enough. "I missed you like crazy." He moved down her luscious body and noticed that she was more voluptuous. How had she become sexier?" He ran his callused palms over her naked flesh and let his thumbs swipe across her nipples, causing her to shudder. All the fear that he'd felt before he laid eyes on her last night had quickly transformed into acute sexual desire.

He got rid of their robes and slid his hand between her folds and discovered how wet she was.

"Max, quit playing around, I'm ready."

"Your wish is my command." He pushed into the tight restrictiveness that he loved and heard her moan in response. Taking a second stroke, he seated himself as a bead of sweat dripped off his brow. Her legs went around his waist as he pushed against her again and felt her wet welcoming heat. "Open your eyes. Look at me, baby." She did as he commanded and let a smile form on her lips. "I sure missed you."

"Yes," she moaned as she tilted her hips.

Taking the hint for what it was, he increased the tempo of his long hard thrusts and felt her tighten around him in response. He gave one final push and exploded, filling her with his seed. A thousand bright lights filled his vision as Rory held him close.

He knew the feelings he had for her were a little insane and hoped with time that Rory would understand how very much he cherished her. "I love you." Lifting his head, he saw a single tear run down her face. "Are you okay?"

"I'm just really emotional lately. Don't pay any attention."

"That's never going to be possible." He rolled off and pulled her against his chest. "I'm glad that you're okay."

"Thank you for flying across the country. I'm glad that you didn't bring the team along to rescue me from whatever bug I've caught."

Smiling against her hair, he decided that keeping the details to himself was best.

"Is this where I don't ask questions that I don't want answers to?"

"Yes." He stroked her back and hoped she left it because the last thing he needed to explain was that he had a fire team ready to respond. It was a measured response as far as he was concerned since he didn't request an entire squad. "How are you feeling? Do you want to go shopping before your doctor's appointment?"

"Do we have time?"

"Let me look up where the doctor's office is."

"I'm going to take a shower so let me know when I return."

He watched her walk into the bathroom and tried to determine what had changed about her figure. Despite her illness, her figure was lush and too freaking delicious to resist.

And since he didn't have any reason to deny himself, he got out of bed and whistled all the way to the bathroom.

It was going to be an incredible day in Florida.

CHAPTER SEVENTEEN

They strolled around the Bal Harbour shopping center and found one of Rory's favorite shops: La Perla. "You're going to enjoy this store. They won't let you in the dressing room, but you can sit in the chair and dream about what I may be buying."

"I don't mind this shopping thing after all. Is this what you do when you go to the mall…buy bras and panties?"

"Not all the time, but I'll make sure to invite you when I do." They stepped into the store, and Rory looked around as Max took a chair. Once she had a pile of possibilities amassed, she blew him a kiss and was surprised that the completely feminine environment made him all the more handsome.

When her usual size didn't fit, she asked a sales associate to measure her. "I don't understand. I've worn the same size since high school."

"Perhaps, you're pregnant. We see this a lot when a woman is in her first trimester."

Rory shook her head. "I don't believe that's possible."

The saleslady nodded. "Let's get you fitted for two bras, just in case. If you're pregnant, these won't last you long."

Smiling blankly, she attempted to process the information as she tried on two bras. Once she found two that fit, she stepped out and went in search of Max. "I'm ready."

"Okay." He stood and held her arms. "Are you okay? You look as pale as a ghost."

"I just need some ginger ale. My stomach is unsettled."

"Okay, let me take care of this, and then we'll grab a drink."

She shook her head. "You can't buy my clothes."

"Sure, I can." He strode to the counter and handed over his credit card.

Wishing she had more energy to make a stand, she let out a sigh and tried to remember the dates of her last cycle.

Max returned with a bag, and she took his hand. "Thank you for the treat."

"Just the beginning."

That's what she was afraid of. Following him to a snack cart, she did her best to ignore the panic that was making itself known.

After they were settled on a bench, she guzzled her soda and tried to recount the days.

"What happened in the dressing room that has you freaked out?"

She turned and let out a breath. "The saleslady said the funniest thing when she was fitting me for a new bra."

"Funny good or funny bad?"

"I'm not sure. She asked if I was pregnant. Isn't that ridiculous? She said needing a larger bra without gaining weight is a common sign of pregnancy."

When a silly smile filled his hard face, she looked away. "I've been under a lot of stress, and I think that's why I missed a cycle." She heard him snort. "It's possible."

Max took Rory's hand. "This isn't how I planned on asking you. I wanted to give you a special romantic evening, but it looks like it would be best to scrub that plan and do it now."

"No asking, Max. There is nothing that we need to decide and…"

His finger went against her lips, and he shook his head. "I want you to know without a doubt that I want to do this regardless of the pregnancy test results. I've been planning this…before I even considered a baby as a possibility."

Was it possible for one's heart to explode in the middle of the prettiest mall in Miami? "Max, we haven't even completed our negotiations. We still have rules of engagement to discuss."

"And we will."

She let her shoulders drop. "We don't have to make promises about the future."

"I'm asking you before we go to the doctor's office."

"You're going to ask me at the shopping center?"

"Yes, we have to leave for the doctor's office in an hour. I want to be on record that I asked you before finding out anything. I also expect your answer to stick, no matter what we find out."

"Well, at least ask me in Neiman Marcus—that way, I'll have a good story to tell people."

"Okay, let's go. Where is it?"

"Right over there." He pulled her up and hustled her along to the store. "I was kidding. We can't…I mean…let's just…"

"Nope. It's happening."

They walked inside, and Rory spotted the shoe department and led him over. They stood in front of the shoes, and she smiled as she looked at the displays. "This is my happy place. If I ever need to escape mentally, this is where I go."

"Good to know." Max flicked his hand out. "Is there any particular area that you like?"

She saw the table filled with Chanel and decided it was the best option since it would set the right tone: classic, elegant, always in style. "I'm going to have to go with the classic Chanel table."

"Good enough." He led her over. "Is this all right?"

"Yes." She picked up a pair of gold sandals that were to die for. "These are gorg."

The salesman approached. "Anything I can help you with?"

"Not yet," Rory replied with a smile. "My boyfriend is going to ask me something first. When he's done, I'd love to try these in size 39."

"Excellent."

Max raised an eyebrow. "Would you like to do some more shopping, or are you ready?"

"No, I'm good. How does my hair look? It's not sticking up or anything?"

"No, you look perfect."

She kissed him gently on the cheek. "Oh wait, I want a picture of this." She got out her phone and waved to the salesperson. "Would you mind taking a couple of photos?"

"Of course, my pleasure."

She straightened her dress and stood up tall. "I'm ready."

"Are you sure?"

She winked. "I've never been more sure of anything in my life."

He leaned down and kissed her before he got down on one knee.

Not able to stop the tear that rolled down her cheek, she wiped it away quickly.

Max looked up and took her hands. "I knew from the first day that I met you that you were the one for me. Hell, I probably knew within the first several hours, and every moment since has confirmed my initial feelings. I love you completely, madly, and desperately, and will spend the rest of my life with your happiness as my first priority."

Swallowing a sob, she nodded.

"How are you doing?"

"Couldn't be better."

"Great...where was I...."

"You love me..."

"I do and would be honored if you would become my wife." He pulled a ring out of his pocket and waited.

Through her tears, she was able to get out her answer in a small voice. "Yes."

He slipped the ring on. "You said yes, right?"

She pulled him up and gave him the kiss of a lifetime. "I would be honored to become your wife."

"Damn right," he shouted as he hugged her tightly.

A round of applause erupted from the Saturday afternoon shoppers, and Rory decided there had never been a better engagement in the history of the world. She lifted her hand and stared at the ring. "You really were going to ask me; you didn't make that up."

"I really was. I love you, Rory Basso, and am damn happy that you're going to marry me."

She admired the ring and was pleased that he'd chosen an emerald since it was her favorite stone. "Thank you, Max."

"I chose this ring because it reminded me of the first time, I met you and saw your pretty eyes. I thought to myself...she has eyes the color of emeralds, and she's going to be a whole lot of trouble."

"I guess we'll see how much when we go to the doctor's office."

"Bring it because I'm more than ready." He gave her a confident wink. "I can't wait to see if my mighty SEAL swimmers did their job and made it to home base."

Before she could respond, the sales associate returned with her phone. "Thank you."

"I got a couple of good photos and a video as well. Do you still want to try on the sandals?"

"I don't need to try them on. You can wrap them up. I'm going to get married in them."

"Excellent."

And Rory thought it was just that.

***

Rory ate sour gummies as she sat in the waiting room of the doctor's office. Max watched her devour almost the whole bag. "How are you doing, baby?"

"Freaking out, thank you for asking."

"Do you want me to go in with you?"

"Of course, you're the one responsible for putting me here. You have to hold my hand when we get the news."

"I'd love nothing more." He watched the nurse approach. "Go time. Let's go meet baby Bishop." When she didn't respond, he decided that it was probably best. A person could only handle so much good news at a time.

Thirty minutes later, they sat in the examination room, and Rory twisted her hair and fidgeted. "How long can it take to look at the results?"

"It hasn't been that long. Remember, they're running blood tests as well."

"What do you think they're going to tell us?"

"That you're pregnant. At least that's what I'm hoping."

"Don't you want to wait for a little while and make sure we're going to be well-suited for one another?"

"You already said that you would marry me and that you love me. I'm not letting you renege on a promise. This is it—we're going to be together for the rest of our lives."

"Okay, fine. I did buy the shoes, after all. It would be a shame to waste them."

He rolled his eyes. "Yeah, that would be tragic."

She squeezed his hand. "Don't pay attention…to my nonsense…I love you and am just freaking out a little."

"I love you, too. Whatever happens, we have each other."

"Together."

The doctor finally returned with a file and a smile. "I have good news. You don't have a stomach virus—you're quite healthy. It appears that your nausea is caused by your pregnancy. The initial blood work suggests that your hormone levels are quite high. That's why your symptoms seem extreme. This could be a sign that you're pregnant with twins. That can't be confirmed until around ten weeks with ultrasound, though."

Rory stared at the doctor in shock. "So, you're sure that I'm pregnant?"

"Yes, I'm sure."

Max bounced to his feet and shook his hand in the air. "That's what I'm talking about." He embraced Rory. "I love you, baby. Thank you for making me the happiest man in the world."

She returned the hug and erupted in laughter. "I guess this is what happens when you get involved with a SEAL. Your swimmers must have super strength."

They heard the doctor laugh. "Come to my office when you're done, and I'll give you some instructions that you can follow until you meet with your doctor at home."

They heard the door close as they stared at each other. "Good thing I got you to agree to marry me. When can we have the wedding?"

"After the baby is born. I'm going to be a little busy over the next seven months."

"No way! We're getting married before the baby comes. I don't want my child to think that I did not want to marry *his* mom."

"I don't believe *she* will think that at all. *She* will understand why we waited."

"No waiting, Rory. We're going to get married soon."

"We're not going to decide right now. Let's go see what the doctor has to say."

He nodded his agreement but knew that he was going to find a way to get married before they left the state. It shouldn't be all that difficult.

***

Several hours later, they were lying on lounge chairs at the beach. "I'm going into the water to cool off before I take a nap," Rory announced. "Do you want to come with me?"

"Of course, I'm not going to let you go in the ocean without me."

"Is this how it's going to be for the next seven months?" she asked with exasperation.

"Maybe...probably. I already feel crazy protective over you, and now you can double or triple that since you're carrying our children."

They strolled down to the water, and Rory noticed all the looks that Max was getting from the women on the beach. She didn't blame them since he was built like a Greek god. He moved with athletic grace, each muscle moving as it was meant to. No doubt, she was a lucky woman and not just because he was physically beautiful. It was his soul that made him a standout.

When their feet hit the surf, Rory let out a sigh. "I miss the feel of a warm ocean."

"I sometimes forget that the ocean can feel so good. I'm so used to our cold temperatures in San Diego." They swam past the break, and Max watched Rory flip over and float on her back. "Feels good, doesn't it?"

"This is such a treat. It feels so relaxing. I could stay out here forever."

"Sounds good to me." He leaned down and ran his mouth down her neck, and then kissed her belly. "Thanks for agreeing to marry me and for the babies."

She opened her eyes and let her legs drift slowly to the sand beneath her feet. "Can we just say baby until we know for sure?"

"Sure. Is two too much to consider right now?"

She took a step forward and wrapped her arms around his neck. "I want to just think about one for a couple of weeks. If I think about two, and then it's only one, I don't want to feel like we lost something."

"Okay, I understand. We have one, and that's a lot to be thankful for." He looked down with tenderness.

"Come here, sailor." She tightened her hands around his neck, savoring the feel of his big muscles. "Kiss me." Melting into him, she met his mouth for a kiss. Her body started signaling pleasure as he held her, and she gave into it.

"We need to go up to the room before I take you in front of everyone."

"That doesn't sound like a bad idea. The doctor may have been right about my hormones."

He laughed as they walked to shore. "Just stay in front of me until we get to our chairs. I'm sporting the evidence of how much my hot fiancée affects me."

She did what he asked as they walked back to their chairs. "Give me a minute while I sit here having some bad and sad thoughts. I need to get myself together, and then we can go upstairs." She smiled as she dried off and combed out her hair. "Please don't look at me like that, either. That's not helping."

She turned around and tried not to laugh as she put on her sunglasses and hat. She dug in her bag for her sour gummies and proceeded to eat them as she sipped from a bottle of water. "I need to go to the gift shop before we go upstairs. I'm almost out of gummies."

"Is this a new obsession?"

"Yes. They are the only thing that helps my stomach, and I don't want to find out what happens when I've run out."

"I'll buy you a case when we get home."

"See, you're already a good husband."

"Speaking of that, how would you feel about a beach wedding?"

"My family would kill us if they missed it, and so would yours."

"Can we have two weddings? I want our anniversary to be close to the baby's conception date. I know it's old-fashioned, but it's important."

"Are you asking me to marry you this week?"

"Yes. I would like nothing more than to take a week off and enjoy your company and get married."

"Alright."

"Are you serious?"

"Yes." She shook her head. "I know it's crazy, but what the heck…"

"That's just the spirit we need. We're on a wild ride, and the best thing we can do is take our hands off the wheel and enjoy it."

"I'll try."

He moved to her side. "That's all I care about. Let's give this our everything and make a family that we're both proud of."

"Okay, Max." Mentally, she threw in the towel and decided that following her warrior into the unknown was her next best move.

CHAPTER EIGHTEEN

Rory watched Max pull up in front of the hotel in the car that he'd rented and wondered if he had a latent desire to become a flashy mogul. She studied the glossy SUV and tilted her head. "Are you sure they didn't have something bigger?"

"I love me a big truck since I'm close to six foot four." Throwing a world-class wink, he rocked back on his heels. "You got any objections, Mrs. Bishop."

She studied the shiny black Escalade and then pursed her mouth. "To the car, no. To your assumption that I'm going to take your name, maybe."

He swept open the door to the car. "You give me an hour and I bet that I can change your mind."

Leaning forward, she moved her mouth to his ear. "Did you get me some sour gummies?"

"A whole, case."

Dragging her mouth down his neck, she smiled against his warm skin. "Then consider the name change, officially under review."

"I appreciate it."

Laughing, she kissed him firmly. And then did it again for good measure since he was more than she ever expected to have. Max Bishop was worth the gamble, and she was ready to make a choice based on hope and not fear. "I'm happy that I decided to marry you."

"Me, too."

She adjusted her caftan and watched her future husband jog around the car and decided that love at first sight wasn't the crazy fairy tale in the book.

An hour later, they flew down the Overseas Highway with the music playing and the ocean breeze flowing through the windows. "I feel pretty relaxed for a woman who is marrying a man who she's only known for two months."

"I've never felt better. I feel like I'm getting everything I want and more."

"I'm going to take a page from your book and lean in."

"Let's take this week and enjoy ourselves as much as we can. When we go home next week, reality will be waiting for us, and there is no need to pretend otherwise."

"You're right." She leaned back against the seat and looked out the window at the ocean as the breeze brushed against her skin. "I love Florida. I used to come down in the summers and play tennis at the Bollettieri Academy. I had a shot at becoming a star of the Junior Tennis circuit before my girl parts came in, and it no longer was a realistic goal."

"I had no idea you liked tennis so much."

"That's going to be the fun part of the next several years. We get to learn all about each other and not be one of those couples that sit at dinner with nothing to talk about."

"Tell me about your tennis career."

"I started playing when I was nine or ten and loved it. I thought that's what I wanted to do for the rest of my life. My parents let me go to the academy when I was twelve. It was heaven. I played tennis all day and got to hang out with kids my age during the evening. I played until I was fifteen before I decided to give it up."

"Do you regret your decision?"

"No, I was as good as I was ever going to get and puberty did me a favor. I returned to California, played on the high school team, and got to be a star in a very small pond."

"I've never really played tennis. Maybe you can teach me."

She looked down at her stomach and then at him. "It may have to wait since we're going to have our hands full."

"I guess you're right." He took her hand.

"So, what's your sports story?"

"Football."

"That's it?"

"I played football from the time I was ten until I graduated college. Some people thought I would try and go pro, but that was never something I was interested in since I had my eye on the military."

"How did you know that the service was the right place for you?"

"When we were little, my dad read us books about war and struggle. Those stories were filled with tales of individual hardship and adventure. The hero was always being tested in some profound way, and all of those stories planted ideas in my head—ideas that never left. I was born a warrior and just needed to find the right home. Sports allowed me to build my self-confidence and sense of identity since I was a hyper-competitive kid. I always pushed myself as hard as I could and constantly looked for the next challenge to beat. I was the kid who felt comfortable being in charge and was often chosen as the captain of any team I was on. Maybe it was because I was the oldest of four boys. I always wanted to be the lead guy and loved to see who had the most guts. That theme played out until I joined the Navy. The idea of seeking adventure, honor, and glory always appealed to me. I was drawn to the SEAL mythology and wanted to be part of a brotherhood that would allow me to get up every day and put everything on the line, including my life. I was lucky enough to find a group of men who were just like me. So yeah, football was my sport."

"You've recreated the brotherhood with your company and doing much the same work with a lot of the same people."

"That was the idea behind it."

"You've succeeded and are doing good work with people you respect in a way that honors the years of service that you gave this country."

"That's the third nicest thing you've said to me. Thank you."

"What was the second?"

"When you told me that you loved me. I didn't expect it. When I flew down here, I just wanted to keep you safe and get a second chance. I had no idea that I was going to win the lottery."

"I'm not the lottery."

"Yes, you are."

She looked out the window and wiped a tear that started to roll down her cheek.

"Would you like to know where we're going?"

Sniffling, she nodded. "Sure."

"We're going to the Little Palm Island Resort, and I hope you love it. I have everything planned, and all you have to do is relax."

"Oh, Max, thank you. I'm so excited."

"Me, too. I can't think of anything better than seven days with the woman of my dreams."

And the man of dreams, I never dared consider. How had she gotten so fortunate?

CHAPTER NINETEEN

The following day, Rory stood at the door with her bag. "I'm leaving." She watched Max walk out of the bedroom with a disgruntled look on his face. "Why the frown."

"I'm going to miss you." He took her hand. "Do you want me to go over there with you?"

"No, we have already broken all kinds of traditions by spending the day together." She cupped his face. "If you want to escape, now is your chance."

He tugged her in and kissed her hotly, devouring her mouth. "Not on your life. I can't believe you agreed to marry me."

"What the heck. It's not like I had anything else planned this afternoon." She patted his chest and stepped back. "I might as well pledge my heart and life to you since we're here."

Letting out a bark of laughter, he shook his head. "I guess that I should count myself lucky that your schedule was free."

"Indeed."

"Don't forget, the photographer will meet you at the spa for a few pictures, and then follow you to the beach."

She leaned up and kissed him. "See ya later, handsome."

"I'll be the one standing next to the minister with a big smile on my face."

"And I'll be the one walking toward you in a white dress." She gathered her things and headed for the spa. Letting out a contented sigh, she couldn't wait to be buffed and polished to bridal perfection. Was it strange that she was so relaxed? Probably not since they'd escaped the wedding madness. A blessing all around since being pregnant was exhausting.

She rubbed her hand over her expanding waist and decided to focus on the pampering she was about to enjoy. And the incredible man she was going to marry.

Not the millions of things she had to get done before she gave birth and figured out to be married to a man who loved harder than she thought possible.

Many hours later, Rory strolled through the lovely resort grounds and tried to take everything in as she made her way to the beach. She was relaxed after the last several hours in the spa and was ready to see her fiancé. The photographer was taking pictures as she walked, which made her feel a little silly, but she decided that at some point, she'd be grateful for the photos.

When she stood at the edge of the sand, she admired her husband to be and knew in her heart that she had made the right choice. No matter what came their way, he would be at her side, standing strong and protecting the family.

Hearing the first notes of music let her know it was time—time to walk toward the man who wasn't going to be easy by any measure but so worth it. She began walking toward her future and saw his hand go to his heart when he caught sight of her. "I made a good choice."

She joined him at the altar and took his hand. "I'm sure glad I didn't have any other plans this afternoon. I would've hated to miss this."

Max let out a big laugh and leaned down, giving her a quick kiss. They heard the minister clear his throat, and they both turned toward him. "Let's get you two married first. Then you can kiss each other for the rest of your lives."

Rory held onto Max's hand and squeezed. "I'm ready if you are?"

"I was ready two months ago."

She turned toward the minister. "Let's get started."

***

"Mrs. Bishop, would you like any more ginger ale?"

"No, thank you, Mr. Bishop." She laughed and lifted her glass to his in a toast. "You sure know how to put on a wedding."

"Thanks, there's still more to come."

"Are you talking about me…later on, this evening?"

"Why, yes, Mrs. Bishop. I plan on fulfilling my husbandly duties many, many times." He liked all the laughter in her eyes and was happy to see that the strain had finally lifted off her shoulders.

"I know you're going to think this is strange but I'm actually glad that I had a stalker." She held up her hand as he was about to protest. "If that was the price that I had to pay to meet you, then it was completely worth it. I know that I'm saying this after everything is over but standing on the beach with you at sunset and pledging our lives to each other made it completely worth it."

"I'm going to agree, but I could've lived without seeing a man with a knife in his hand in your office."

"But look at us now. Whatever brought us to this moment was *worth* it."

Waiters approached with dinner as they sat on their private beach with tiki torches surrounding them and music playing in the background. They were served a delicious meal in complete privacy as the waves lapped at the shore and the smell of sea salt-washed over them. "I can't thank you enough for an amazing day. Rory took his hand. "You gave me all the best parts of a wedding without the pain and agony of a big hoopla."

"Mrs. Bishop, I would like you to tell me five things that you want from me over the next fifty or sixty years. I want your list of things I can do to make you happy."

"Max, that's a lot of pressure. Can I give you a couple of things and then add to the list later on?"

"How about if we keep one at home and change it as it becomes necessary? It will become the living, breathing direction of our marriage. It's bound to change over the years. Let's keep it up on the fridge— that way, we are conscious of it daily. Something to aspire to, a goal to work on."

"That is a brilliant idea." She folded her hands. "Okay, these are just off the top of my head."

"I'm ready."

"Excellent. I want you to keep kissing and hugging me whenever the thought crosses your mind. I don't want you to stop doing that. And tell me how you feel, whether you think I'm going to like it or not. And I want you to laugh at my jokes, no matter how bad they are, and trust me enough to give me space."

"What else?"

"If your feelings change, I want you to tell me first."

"I can do that."

"Tell me yours."

"The first thing that I would like is for you to keep looking at me the same way you did when you were walking down the aisle today. Hold me tight when you sleep; that's one of my favorite things. And turn to me when you need something and tell me how you feel. Always."

"I can do that."

"I have a wedding present for you but can't give it to you until we get home."

"How did you have time to organize a present?"

"I got this for you last month in hopes that we could enjoy it together. I had no idea that we would get married down here."

"I didn't get you anything yet."

He put his hand on her stomach. "Oh, yes, you did. You're making me the best present in the world."

"I'm going to think of something else to go with it."

"Not necessary. Today was the best day of my life."

"Me, too. I'm getting a little tired, though. Are you ready to go in?"

"Absolutely." They walked up the beach into their suite, and Rory lost her breath. There were tiny candles scattered around the room, and there was a path of rose petals leading into the bedroom. Max picked her up and carried her over the threshold of the bedroom, and kicked the door closed with his foot. "Mrs. Bishop, would you like to consummate this marriage?"

She let her feet hit the ground and looked around the room at a scene that was worthy of a movie. She turned and let the clasp from her dress free. It slithered down her body, and she was left standing in her pretty La Perla thong and nothing else. "I guess I am."

He let out a growl, swept her up, and gently laid her on the bed that was scattered with rose petals. "I love you."

"Love you more."

CHAPTER TWENTY

A week later, Jackson sat in his office and tried to decide if the rumors he kept hearing were true. It was hard to believe that his father would sell the hotels without talking to him. The only way it might be possible was if he thought he was using again.

I don't think that's likely. I'm totally under control this time.

Did Rory know anything about it? He wished that he still had access to her phone and computer. Her leaving the company had eliminated his only source of information regarding his father's plans.

Gavin's arrest and betrayal had hit him hard. The guy had completely thrown him under the bus. And because things could always get worse, the detective seemed to believe the guy's story. Not that anything could be proved. It was going to be his word against someone guilty of pulling a knife on his step-sister.

Unfortunately, his dad blamed him for what happened to Rory. Wiping the film of sweat covering his neck, he let out a disgusted breath. It was just like his father not to believe him; he always blamed Jackson for things.

The brutal conversation with his father still rang in his head. Why couldn't the man be on his side for once? And what had made him trust Rory more than him? He'd love to know how the bitch accomplished it.

Realizing that the how and why were not immediately important, he focused on the most pressing matter. He needed some information on the timeline of the sale.

Maybe it was time to pay a visit and see if the mighty Rory could divulge some clues.

She'd probably gotten over the Gavin thing and was ready to do him a solid and share what she knew. The only obstacle he could see would the boyfriend. Max wasn't a forgiving guy and was way too overprotective.

Whatever. How much trouble could the guy be?

***

Rory was thrilled to be back home in her cozy little house. "Can you open all the windows in the living room?"

"Are you sure you want to open everything?" Max asked. "The storm may be coming in tonight."

She walked into the living room with a pile of clothes for the dry cleaners. "I want to air the house out before the rain comes. It's been closed for almost a month."

"I forgot it was that long. You took two and half weeks to travel to all of the offices, and then we were in Florida for almost two weeks."

"I need to go to the grocery store. Are you going to your office to check in?"

"I was going to wait until tomorrow." He opened the French doors to the patio. "If you give me a list, then I'll go to the market."

"Okay, that sounds good. I can get myself organized and start the laundry." She pressed a kiss to her husband's cheek and decided that matrimony wasn't half bad. Not only was Max easy to look at, but he was helpful too. "I'm going to crash early since

I'm still on Florida time. How does risotto and a salad sound?"

"Perfect." He bent down and cupped her jaw. "Just like my wife."

"Are you going to slip that into conversation whenever you can?"

"Probably," he replied with a chuckle. "I may forget your name entirely and just call you wife or Mrs. Bishop."

"I prefer Mrs. Bishop. You can only call me wife when we're in bed, and you ask me for sexual favors."

He pressed a gentle kiss against her mouth. "So 'wife' will soon be associated with pleasure in your mind."

"It already is."

"Guess that means, I should start thinking about which one I want to ask for first."

"Yeah," Rory said with a laugh. "Careful consideration might be a good idea."

"What about you, what kind of favors would you like to ask for?"

"I can't think of one thing that you haven't already done, Mr. Bishop; I'm pretty easy to please."

"What are you saying?" He stepped back and frowned. "Do you think that we need to be more daring?"

"No, I'm saying that I married a man who is better than any dream I could've come up with on my own. That says more about me than anything else." He pulled her forward and let his lips fall against hers. The kiss went from a slow, gentle expression of their love to lust in less than a minute. That must be why people called it the honeymoon phase.

Several minutes later, Max pulled back and sucked in a breath. "I'd better go to the grocery store before I lose all control and take you into the bedroom."

She fluttered her eyes and slowly pulled herself out of a lust-induced fog. "If you give me a minute, to get my mind right, I'll make a list."

"Take all the time you need." He kissed her head and winked before walking out of the kitchen.

Tearing her eyes away, she laughed. "I am the luckiest woman in the world."

Thirty minutes later, Rory stood in her kitchen and realized that everything about her life had changed since the last time she stood there. She had walked out of her house thirty days ago and wasn't sure if she was going to continue to see Max. Now, she was married and pregnant. What a difference a month made! Shaking her head, she started to collect the ingredients for the risotto and heard her phone buzz. Pulling it out, she read the text from Birdie welcoming her home and a demand for all the information about her trip. If Birdie saw her, she would figure everything out. It would take one look from her best friend for her to know that she was pregnant and married. *How long can I hide out before I confess everything?*

She quickly texted her back and suggested lunch for the following week. That might just give her the time she needed. Her phone started buzzing again, and it was an e-mail from the manager of the Hotel Valencia confirming availability for the ceremony on Sunday. Was it foolish to try and pull off a second wedding for the family? Possibly, but what could she do? Their families would be furious if they missed out on celebrating their happy union.

Not wanting to dive into the mental to-do list the event required, she turned her attention to preparing dinner.

Once the risotto was bubbling away, she stirred it slowly and added a cup of warm chicken broth. Contented to be in her favorite place, she was surprised to hear a sound on the patio. Was the neighbor's cat was chasing something in the backyard again? Dismissing it, she continued to stir and enjoy the pitter-patter of light rain.

The sound of the screen door scraping open startled her and she dropped the spoon, twirling around. "What in the world?" Her hand flew to her chest, and she had a bad feeling that the arrival of a sweaty, disheveled Jackson was not good news. Especially since his eyes were dilated as he glanced around frantically. "So, you don't like to use the front door. Something wrong with knocking, Jackson?"

Her heart beat out of her chest, and she knew remembering where she stashed her gun was important. Unfortunately, the cortisol rushing through her system made it all but impossible. Praying to her favorite saint, she asked for Max's quick return.

"Shut up, Rory. I know what you did."

"That's rude; you can't come into my home and tell me to shut up. Why are you sneaking around and coming in through the backyard?" A dumb question? Absolutely. But she needed to stall for as much time as she could.

"I didn't want your cameras to record my image."

"Well, too bad for you there are cameras everywhere." She shook her head. "Did you really think that Max would leave me unprotected?"

"Whatever."

Brilliant comeback! Pushing herself to her full height, she slowly felt anger replace fear. "Did you think you were going to get away with asking a deranged man to stalk me?"

"I didn't ask Gavin to stalk you."

Letting out a loud snort, she wondered if he believed his own drivel. "We both know what you did and that you're ultimately responsible for what happened in my office."

"I didn't pull the knife and attempt to kidnap you."

"No, you were just the one who asked a mentally unstable man to keep an eye on me."

"It's over. Forget about it."

As if that was possible. "What are you doing here?"

"You have to tell me what you know about the rumor of the sale of the hotels."

"I don't work there anymore. Why do you think that I know anything?"

"Because you know everything, and your mother would tell you if something was going on."

"I can't help you."

"I don't believe you."

"I don't care." She fisted her hands on her hips. "If you would like to survive the evening, I suggest you leave. Max is minutes away and won't be happy with your presence."

Jackson took a step closer. "You screwed everything up. It's all falling apart, and it's your fault."

"That's ridiculous! And makes no sense."

"All the deals that I have in place are going to fall apart if there is a sale of the hotels."

"Call your father."

"He's not taking my calls; he's pissed about what happened to you."

"Imagine that. What a shock."

"I don't appreciate your attitude."

"I don't appreciate you breaking into my house. You need to leave right now."

"No, you need to fix this!"

She tried to determine the level of insanity he was committed to. Was he experiencing a psychotic breakdown, or was he just strung out on something? "Do you want me to call your father and ask him?"

He looked around wild-eyed as if he were trying to come up with an answer. "You need to come with me and talk to the people that I cut the deal with. They might believe you because they think you know what's going on."

"That doesn't make any sense. Go home, Jackson. I'm not going anywhere with you."

He took a step forward and grabbed her arm. "I said that I want you to come with me."

She tried to get him to release his grip. "Let. Me. Go. Do you know what Max is going to do to you when he walks in the door?"

"I don't care about Max. You need to come with me now!" He gripped her arm and started to pull her away from the stove.

Digging her heels in, she resisted. She had seen enough crime shows to know that you never left with an attacker. "Max will kill you if you've scared me or uttered a rude word in my direction. Escape while you can because I won't be able to stop him. Not that I want to since I'm over your nonsense."

"I don't care; you're coming with me."

"No!" She was tired of men threatening her and thinking they had some agency over her person. Yanking her arm out of his grip, she placed one hand on the handle of the pan with risotto. Grateful that she had invested in the heavy-bottomed saucepan, she lifted it in one easy motion. "Go to hell, Jackson!"

He tried to lunge for her, and she swung the saucepan in an arc, letting it smash against his head. The hot risotto slid down his head as he dropped to the floor.

Was he dead?

She'd told Max that she was going to smash the bastard's head in when she found out who was responsible, and she had.

The door flew open, and Max ran in with his gun drawn. "What the hell happened?"

Rory stood in the middle of her beautiful kitchen with a big pan in her hand, staring down at the floor. "I might've killed him. I hit him really hard on the head." She looked up with tears streaming down her face. "I'm tired of men attempting to hurt me and trying my last nerve. I should call 911."

Rushing over, he swept her into his arms as she collapsed against him. Engulfing her, he gently removed the pan from her fingers and set it down. "I called 911 when I saw the breach on the backyard gate." He tightened his hold. "You became your own hero and saved your own life, sweetheart." He pressed a kiss to her head. "If I was an insecure man, I might worry that you don't need me."

She started to laugh. Burying her face in his chest, she tried to disappear into him. "Holidays are definitely going to be awkward if Jackson shows up at any of them. It's going to take me a long time to forgive him for this."

"No doubt." The cops and paramedics came rushing in the door, and the chaos began. "How are you feeling? We should go to the hospital and have you and the baby checked out. I want to make sure that you're both okay."

She nodded. "That might be a good idea."

Two hours later, Rory lay in the hospital bed attached to all kinds of monitors. "Max, did you bring my sour gummies?"

He pulled a bag out of the pocket of his sweatshirt. "Here you go. Are you sure it's okay if you have them now?"

"Are you sure that you want to stay married?" Narrowing her eyes, she held out her hand. "Pass them over and no one else will get hurt."

"I see how it's going to be with you," he said with a smile.

"I've had a rough evening and want my candy."

He opened the bag, handed them to her, and kissed her on the head. "I should have been aware of where Jackson was when we got home."

"I don't think there was anything that you could've done." She patted his hand. "Look at all you've accomplished in just a month and a half." She pressed the bag of candy to her chest. "You've protected me, married me, and managed to knock me up." Pulling him close, she let out a breath. "You're definitely a man who can multi-task."

The door slid open, and Carolina walked in. "Well, *cara*, it seems that you've had a difficult evening." She kissed her daughter's head. "Is there something you want to tell me?"

Max stood. "We have some great news for you. You're going to be excited about it."

"When is my grandchild going to be born?"

"We look forward to welcoming the baby in June," he said quietly.

Carolina gave Max a slow once over. "I see." Taking her daughter's hand and Max's, she held them together. "Anything else you would like to share with me? I'm guessing that you did more than swim and lay on the beach in Florida."

Rory tried to sit up but was hampered by all the monitors that she was attached to. "Mama."

"Don't 'Mama' me, Rory Evangeline Basso. You're in trouble."

"Mama, we're going to have another ceremony this weekend, and you will be there to see it."

Max stepped forward. "This was my idea. I wanted to get married right away so our anniversary would be close to the baby's conception date. I never wanted there to be any question that we were not together in every way."

"I understand, but I'm going to be mad for a little while. I know that so much has been going on since Jackson started all of this craziness. Let me ask you this, Max Bishop, do you love my daughter?"

"With my whole heart. For the rest of my life. She will always be my first priority, as well as the children we have."

"All right, I can live with that," Carolina said with a smile. "All I want for my girls is for them to be happy and loved. You're not getting married again this weekend, though. Let's wait and take our time so we can give people enough time to arrange their travel plans. I want to meet your parents and have time to get to know them. Let's do it right; there's no need to rush."

"All right, Mama, that's a good idea," Rory said with sigh. "Thank you for understanding."

Max hugged Carolina. "Thank you. I know Rory was worried about how you would feel."

"The first priority is Rory's health and the health of the baby. Let's not make stress where we don't have to."

"Mama, I bashed Jackson over the head with my risotto pan."

Her mother studied her for a second with a concerned face and then broke out in a laugh. She quickly covered her mouth and shook her head. "I know it's wrong to laugh, but that boy has had problems for years. In a way, he had it coming for all the pain he's initiated. He's caused his father so much grief and sadness, despite everything he's done for him."

"Maybe he'll get the help he needs and change his life around."

"I hope he does because he's been cut off by his father. Bob set up provisions with his lawyer that Jackson has to meet. If he's unable to do that, then he will not be eligible for any of the money in his trust. It was a smart move because it leaves me out of it. It's between Jackson, the lawyer, and the director of his trust. Bob set it up almost a year ago, along with the sale of his company. When we first got the diagnosis, he confessed that he'd been aware of it for almost two years."

"How are you doing, Mama? Do you feel like you're under a lot of pressure?"

"No, I'm relieved. We have a diagnosis, a plan, and now we just enjoy all the good days we have together. Bob took care of everything before he felt like he was unable to."

They were interrupted by a knock on the door; a tech rolled in a big cart with the ultrasound machine. "Would you like to take a look at baby Bishop?"

"I would love to see the baby," Rory said excitedly.

"My first picture of my grandchild. I'm so lucky to be here."

Max went around to the other side of the bed. "I hope she looks like you." He kissed Rory quickly and then rested his head against her forehead. "Love you."

"Love you more."

The images started to show on the monitor as the tech moved the paddle around on Rory's stomach. "When is your due date?"

"I think they estimated June 15th. How does the baby look in there?"

The woman was quiet as she studied the monitor, and Rory started to feel a flutter of nerves. "You are around ten weeks pregnant. That's a little early to determine if you are having twins. Let's see what's happening."

Max held his breath and wondered if his gut was going to be right about this. The tech continued to move around the monitor and clicked buttons as she created images and noted measurements. She finally smiled. "Mr. and Mrs. Bishop, it's going to be twins."

Max fell into the chair. "Holy shit."

A tear rolled down her cheek. "Show off."

A huge smile creased his face. "I can't help it if my swimmers used their super SEAL strength to make it to home base."

Carolina took both of their hands. "*Congratulazioni! I nostril migliori auguri e tanta felicita.*" She kissed them both and studied the monitor. "I would like to have copies of the pictures as well. These are my first grandchildren, and I've waited a long time."

"Mama, I'm only twenty-eight. You have not been waiting long."

She shrugged her shoulders. "It seemed like a long time."

Rory shook her head. "Well, at least we're giving you two since you had to wait *so* long."

"And I appreciate it."

The tech finished the ultrasound and rolled the cart out and Carolina moved toward the door. "I'm going to let you two have a few minutes alone."

When they were alone Rory engulfed Max in a hug. "You were totally unexpected, Max Bishop." Pressing a kiss on his cheek, she knew that every single one of her prayers had been answered. He was a risk, a mystery, and the most certain thing she'd ever known.

EPILOGUE

"I can't believe that tomorrow is Christmas Eve," Rory exclaimed. "I feel like it was just yesterday that I walked into your office asking for help with my stalker."

They walked toward Birdie and Mark's house when Max stopped in front of a home that was having work done. "That's the house that Birdie and I looked at last month. Someone must have bought it."

Max pulled her through the gate. "Do you want to look inside?"

"No, I don't want to snoop."

"Come on. Let's go see if the door is open."

"Max, stop. We can't."

"Yes, we can." He walked backward, holding both her hands.

She looked at his mischievous smile and started to get an inkling of what was going on. "Mr. Bishop, is there anything that you would like to tell me?"

"There might be something."

"Max, please…"

They stood at the front door, and he pulled out a key ring with a red ribbon. "Merry Christmas, sweetheart."

Speechless, she stared at the key. "You bought me my dream home? How did you know?"

"I remembered how much you loved it. I contacted the realtor the following day and started the process of purchasing it. It closed while you were on your trip."

"We were not even speaking at the time, and you bought a house that you knew I loved."

"I hoped that you would give me another chance and thought this might help. I told you that I wanted everything, and the only way to get that is to give everything."

She lifted the key and saw the sun glint off the surface as it turned in the lock. Max Bishop was a revelation and had brought every magical thing into her life.

They walked in the front door and stood in a puddle of light and looked around their new home. "You're right. Five bedrooms isn't too big at all."

Max took her hand. "Adam is checking out the electrical and plumbing and refinishing some surfaces and painting the walls white. All you have to do is tell him what you want."

"How did you know what to do?"

"I spoke with Birdie, and she gave me some ideas. I'm smart enough to ask if I don't know the answer."

"I'm lucky that I married you."

"We're lucky."

"Let's go upstairs." They made their way up the wide staircase, and Rory stopped for a moment. "Just think, someday we're going to watch our daughter walk down these stairs when she's getting ready to go on her first date, and we're going to hear the loud footsteps of our son when he's on his way outside to play. Everything important in our lives is going to happen in this house."

"Our daughter is not going to date until she graduates college."

She patted his arm as they started moving up the stairs. "Whatever you need to tell yourself to get through the next twenty years."

He followed her up the steps. "I'm serious about the dating thing."

"I know, honey. I know."

They entered the master bedroom, and he held her tightly. "We're going to make a lot of memories in here!" They sat against the wall, facing the big set of windows that looked out over the backyard. "Just think, we're going to make more babies in here."

Rory let out a loud laugh. "Can I deliver the two we have before we talk about anymore?"

"Sure, sweetheart. We'll practice a lot in here. Does that sound better?"

"Yes, practicing is good."

"Do you want to change anything on your top five list yet?"

"No, I'm happy with it. What about you?"

"I'm going to keep mine as well."

She turned with a serious expression on her face. "I want to thank you for making me realize that loving someone could be easy. Loving you is easy."

"I hope that I never do anything to change your mind about that. Remember, you have to tell me if it does."

"I will." She rested her head against his shoulder. "You make me feel beloved, Mr. Bishop, and I didn't even know that was possible."

"You are beloved, Mrs. Bishop. You are *my* beloved, and I plan on spending the rest of my life making sure you know that."

CORONADO SERIES
LATCHED
SNATCHED
ATTACHED
CATCH
FATE
BEWITCHED
HITCHED
SWITCHED
TUMULT
INFATUATED
FASCINATED
COMPLICATED (2022)

SAI SERIES
VORTEX
WHIRLWIND
TEMPEST
BESIEGE
BARRAGE

SPORTS CENTER
SHAKEDOWN
SHOWDOWN
TAKEDOWN
SHOWDOWN (2022)

TROUBLE SERIES
ROGUE
CHAOS
RASCAL
SCOUNDREL
PATRIOT

HAVEN SERIES
TRUST
TEMPTED

LANDRY BROTHERS
IRRESISTIBLE
INEVITABLE

STANDALONE
A WHOLE LOTTA TROUBLE
SMITTEN
UNMATCHED

Lea Hart is a bestselling author of military romance and romantic comedy. She is well known for her steamy sweet, witty novels. She lives in Southern California and manages to keep a firm grasp on her sanity despite the efforts of her teenager. A big glass of wine, the right pair of shoes, and an appreciation for the absurd ensure that the daily juggling act is somewhat successful.